Advanced Play at Bridge

by the same author

KILLING DEFENCE AT BRIDGE
MATCH-POINT BRIDGE
HOW TO IMPROVE YOUR BRIDGE
MORE KILLING DEFENCE AT BRIDGE
LOGICAL BRIDGE PLAY
TEST YOUR MATCH PLAY
THE TOUGH GAME
BRIDGE: THE MIND OF THE EXPERT

ADVANCED PLAY AT BRIDGE

H. W. KELSEY

FABER AND FABER
London & Boston

First published in 1968
by Faber and Faber Limited
3 Queen Square London WC1
Reprinted 1970 and 1973
First published in
Faber Paperbacks in 1981
Printed in Great Britain by
Whitstable Litho Limited, Whitstable, Kent
All rights reserved

British Library Cataloguing in Publication Data

Kelsey, Hugh Walter
Advanced play at bridge
1. Contract bridge
I. Title
795.4'15   GV1282.3

ISBN 0-571-11677-9

For ANNE, GEORGE, JANE and RICHARD

Acknowledgements

I am indebted to Eric Milnes and Messrs. John Waddington for kind permission to use some hands from my articles in *Bridge Magazine*.

My grateful thanks are also due to Denis Young and John MacLaren for making a critical survey of my script, tearing a number of the hands apart, and handing me back the pieces for re-assembly.

H.W.K.

Contents

INTRODUCTION   *page* 13
1. A TIME FOR THINKING   15
2. COUNTING THE HAND   33
3. CARD-PLACING   51
4. CAMOUFLAGE   70
5. GOOD AND BAD BREAKS   89
6. BACKING THE FAVOURITE   111
7. COMMUNICATIONS   131
8. PRESSURE PLAY   150
9. MATCH POINT   180

Introduction

Over the past twenty years so much has been written about dummy play that the reader might be pardoned for wondering if there can be anything fresh to say on the subject. A number of first-class text-books are available to the student, but I believe there are still some aspects of play, mainly in the field of card-reading as opposed to technique, that have not received adequate coverage from the writers. It is on those aspects that I have tried to concentrate in the following pages.

Most of the problems in this book are fresh ones taken from play, but a few have been adapted from various sources and one or two constructed to illustrate a point. Once again the quiz form of layout has been adopted. The reader is shown only twenty-six cards and can attempt to work out the answer to each problem for himself before reading on.

INTRODUCTION

I would like to emphasize here that most of the problems are fairly tough. When you come upon some reference in the text to the logic of a situation being 'clear enough' or 'not too difficult', please bear in mind that I am speaking relatively. None of the problems is really easy, and this is no book for a beginner.

After all, bridge is a difficult game to play well. Any author who pretends otherwise is being unfair to his readers. Nobody need feel discouraged at failing to find the right answers to a lot of the problems in this book. To get as many as 50 per cent of them correct will be very good, 60 per cent will be an excellent score and 70 per cent superlative. Only an expert can expect to come up with the right answer to 80 per cent or more of the problems. And in the heat of play at the bridge table even the expert might not do so well.

The classification of the problems into chapters has been done on a somewhat arbitrary basis, since there are many hands that could fit equally well into any one of several chapters. Running over the headings you may be surprised to see nothing about throw-in or elimination play, but deals illustrating these plays abound in every chapter. Another pervasive theme is that of safety. You will find that the making of the contract is regarded as all-important throughout the book, with the exception of the last chapter which deals with match-point duplicate.

Theoretically, it could be more profitable in the long run to go for overtricks and ignore safety play, but in practice this would be psychologically unsound. At rubber bridge your duty to your partner of the moment is to clinch the rubber by making your contract as safely as possible, while at team-of-four play you owe it to your team-mates not to risk a large adverse swing for the sake of the odd overtrick.

A bidding sequence is given with each problem, but I hope you will not take it that the bidding has my approval in every case. Players do get to unreasonable contracts at times, and the only way to get there is by an unreasonable bidding sequence. So if you don't like the bidding on any deal, please assume you have been asked to play the hand for some crazy declarer who has been called to the telephone. For the purposes of this book the bidding is important only in so far as it helps you to place the opponents' cards.

CHAPTER 1

A Time for Thinking

The bidding is over, your left-hand opponent chooses his opening lead, and dummy is spread on the table before you. This is a hopeful moment of time. No mistake has yet been made. All things are possible. You may earn admiration for the masterly competence of your play, or you may make a complete mess of the hand and end up ashamed to look your partner in the eye. This is the time when contracts are made or lost. It is a time for thinking.

The player does not exist who can lay his hand on his heart and say that he has never been guilty of hasty and careless play to the first couple of tricks. It is one of the commonest faults in the game, and certainly the most expensive. If unchecked it is likely to cost you more tricks than all your other mistakes put together. This is because the first decision you have to make is usually a vital one. If you make a false step at an early stage it will often prove impossible to recover. For that reason it is well worth while taking a little time to think before playing to the first trick.

Don't think I am recommending long trances. The slow, slow players who trance after every trick do the game a great disservice. Most hands are straightforward enough and do not call for a great deal of thought, but when you have a tricky contract to play you are entitled to take the time you need, within reason, to work out the best line of play.

Before touching a card from dummy you should carry out a careful survey of the whole hand, looking out especially for any snags that could develop when you embark on your chosen line of play. You should try to anticipate bad breaks and map out a flexible plan of campaign that will cover as many contingencies as possible.

Basically this is a matter of counting your tricks. When dummy goes down your first task is to add up the top winners contained in the combined hands, for only thus will you be able to calculate the number of extra tricks you need to develop for your contract. There may be several possible ways of developing extra tricks and the choice between different lines of play may be close. At the same time you must make a careful count of your losers and if necessary look for ways of limiting them. In a major suit game contract a sure plan for establishing ten tricks is of little use if it permits your opponent to cash four tricks first.

Perhaps you are wondering why I choose to bore you with such elementary stuff. You are an experienced player. You have heard it all before. You know all about counting your tricks and you wouldn't dream of playing to the first trick before forming a logical plan.

I wonder.

Before we go any further have a look at this hand.

```
          ♠ 7 3
          ♡ K 8
          ◇ Q 8 2
          ♣ K J 6 5 4 2

              N
          W       E
              S

          ♠ A K Q 6
          ♡ A 7
          ◇ A J 9 6 5
          ♣ Q 8
```

Your contract is three no trumps and the opening lead a small heart. How would you plan the play?

Following the basic rule of counting your top tricks, you see that you have three in spades, two in hearts and one in diamonds. You will have to develop three additional tricks in either diamonds or clubs, and you can give up the lead only once before the opponents establish their long hearts.

Three plausible lines of play present themselves for consideration. You could win the first trick with dummy's king and take an immediate diamond finesse, you could win the first trick with the ace of hearts and tackle diamonds from your hand, or you could win with the ace and play on clubs.

This is quite a deceptive hand. It is not too easy to see that nine tricks are always available provided that the diamonds do not break worse than 4–1. The correct method of play is to win the first trick with the ace of hearts and play off the ace of diamonds. If an opponent shows out you will have to switch to clubs, but if both follow you can continue with a small diamond towards the queen. If either opponent wins this trick with the king you must make four diamond tricks and your contract. If West plays low on the second diamond and East shows out when you play dummy's queen you will have to abandon the suit, but with two diamond tricks in the bag you can establish the other two tricks you need in clubs. It takes a combination of a 5–0 diamond break and a 4–1 club break to defeat this line of play.

The hand was played in the English Bridge Union International Trials of 1964, and it is a matter of record that thirteen out of sixteen declarers failed to make three no trumps. The 'unlucky' thirteen won the first trick with the ace of hearts and led the queen of clubs at trick two. Justice was served when the clubs broke 4–1 and the diamond finesse turned out to be wrong.

Now those were not poor players. To receive an invitation to play at the E.B.U. International Trials you have to be a very fine player indeed. Why, then, did so many have the same blind spot in the play?

If you had been present and had made the rounds of the unsuccessful players asking why they had gone down in a stone cold contract, you would have received at every table the same rueful shrug and the reply: 'I played too quickly.'

That is the truth of the matter. It was not that those declarers knew no better. They were quite capable of selecting the superior line of play and well aware of the proper way to handle that diamond combination. But a knowledge of expert technique is of little use if it cannot be applied at the correct time. All thirteen declarers were guilty of the commonest of all mistakes—over-quick analysis. If they had taken an extra ten seconds to study the position they would surely have replaced the queen of clubs in their hands and pulled out the ace of diamonds instead.

Even at this rarefied level, it seems, declarers need to discipline themselves to avoid undue haste and carelessness in playing to the first few tricks.

The problems in this chapter illustrate many different aspects of technique, but they are all hands in which a vital decision has to be taken at an early stage in the play. Don't fail to count your tricks and make a careful, logical plan. If you play too quickly from dummy it may cost you the contract.

A TIME FOR THINKING

♠ A J 9 6 2
♡ A K 4
◇ 7 6
♣ K J 8

Game all

	West	North	East	South
♠ 7 4 3	1 ♡	1 NT	—	3 NT
♡ 6	4 ◇	—	4 ♡	5 ♣
◇ K 5	all pass			
♣ A Q 10 9 6 4 2				

West leads the queen of hearts against your five club contract. How do you plan the play?

It is just as well that you did not press on with four no trumps, for your partner's poor choice of call on the first round had placed the declaration in the wrong hand. You are also lucky to have avoided playing in four spades since on the bidding West must be very short in the black suits. In that case the straightforward method of play—discarding a diamond on the high heart and trying to limit your spade losers to one—is not likely to succeed.

You have chances, of course, if West has the king of spades singleton or doubleton. You could play trumps until West shows out, discard a spade on a high heart and ruff the small heart and then lead a spade towards dummy, ducking if West plays the king. No return by West could now hurt you.

But by far the best line of play is to allow West to hold the first trick. This succeeds whenever the spades break 3–2, and also when they are 4–1 if West does not switch to trumps (and he may well have no trump to lead). On a spade switch you win with the ace, discard your losing spades on the top hearts, and ruff a spade high. Now dummy has enough trump entries for you to establish the fifth spade for a diamond discard.

♠ 10 8 7 6 4 3
♡ K J 7
◇ Q 4
♣ A 8   *Love all*

	South	West	North	East
♠ Q J 9 5 2	1 ♠	—	4 ♠	all pass
♡ A 10 3				
◇ K J 6				
♣ Q 2				

West leads the two of hearts against your four spade contract. How do you plan the play?

Counting your winners, you see that you can establish at least four trump tricks, you have three hearts on this lead, you can set up two diamonds, and the ace of clubs brings your total up to ten. That looks all right, but what about your losers? If the ace and king of trumps are in the same hand is there not a danger that you may lose two spades, a diamond and a club?

In view of this possibility you cannot afford to lead trumps immediately. You must first play on diamonds so as to establish a winner on which to throw dummy's losing club.

Are you in the clear now, or are there any further snags to look out for? The only possible source of complication is that your hand is not too rich in immediate entries. It looks as though West has led away from the queen of hearts, but there is no excuse for carelessness here. If you play the seven of hearts from dummy on the first trick and the queen forces your ace you will be in real trouble. The opponents will hold off until the second round of diamonds and then attack clubs, and you will be unable to get back to your hand in time to avoid losing a club trick.

The proper card to play from dummy at trick one is the knave of hearts. This protects you against any possible entry trouble.

A TIME FOR THINKING

♠ A J
♡ Q 10
◇ K 10 4
♣ A K 8 7 6 3

Game all

	West	North	East	South
♠ 10 6 4 3	—	1 ♣	—	1 ♡
♡ K J 9 8 7 4	—	2 NT	—	3 ♡
◇ 6	—	4 ♡	all pass	
♣ 5 2				

West leads the ace and another diamond. How do you play?

You have nine fairly certain tricks. The tenth could come from clubs if they break 3–2, or spades, or possibly a spade ruff in dummy. The trouble is that if you lead trumps at once West may win the second round and lead a spade, knocking out dummy's ace before it can be used as an entry for the long clubs. And if you play ace and another spade the defenders will counter with two rounds of trumps and again you will be a trick short.

The correct play is to win the second trick with the king of diamonds, discarding a spade from your hand, and lead the knave of spades from the table. This keeps control of the situation by placing the defenders in a dilemma. They can either play two rounds of trumps to stop you ruffing a spade or they can knock out the spade ace, but they cannot do both.

Note that it would not be safe to ruff the second trick in your hand in order to lead towards dummy's spades. On winning with the king or queen of spades East could return a trump which you would be allowed to win. You would have to cash dummy's top tricks and re-enter your hand by ruffing the third round of clubs. But West could over-ruff with the ace and lead another trump, and you would go down to defeat if West started with four trumps.

You need a 3–2 club break to make this contract, but you can and should protect yourself against a 4–1 trump break.

A TIME FOR THINKING

```
♠ Q 9 4 3
♡ 9 7 6 3
♢ K 7 2                    Love all
♣ 5 2
                  South   West   North   East
                  1 ♠     2 ♡    2 ♠      —
♠ A 10 8 6 5 2    4 ♠     all pass
♡ 4
♢ A 6 4
♣ A Q 8
```

West leads the ace of hearts against your four spade contract and East plays the two. West now switches to the knave of diamonds. How do you play?

The immediate problem is how to tackle the trumps. The safety play to avoid losing more than one trump trick in this situation is well known, but this may not be the right time to employ it. You would feel foolish if you gave up an unnecessary trump trick only to find that you had a loser in each of the side suits.

It appears that the club position is the crux of this hand. Is there any way of avoiding the finesse? A throw-in can hardly work even if West has a doubleton diamond and king and another spade, for dummy has not enough entries for you to eliminate the hearts. Nor can the club queen figure as a squeeze menace since you need to ruff a club in dummy.

If the club finesse has to be taken it must be correct to try it before playing trumps, for that will clarify your loser situation. You should win the second trick with dummy's king of diamonds and lead a club at trick three. If West produces the club king you will know that you cannot afford a spade loser and will play the ace of spades on the first round in the hope that someone has a singleton king. If the club finesse is successful, on the other hand, you can afford to play for safety in the trump suit. After ruffing the third round of clubs you will lead a small trump from dummy. If East plays the seven you will make sure of your contract by covering with the ten.

```
♠ K 8 4
♡ 7 3
◇ A J 10 8 2                    Game all
♣ A 6 5
                         South    North
♠ A 9 7 5 2              1 ♠      2 ◇
♡ A 8 5                  2 ♠      4 ♠
◇ 7 3
♣ K J 8
```

West leads the king of hearts against your four spade contract.
Having been trained to avoid hasty play, you give the matter
some thought before playing low from both hands. West now
switches to the four of diamonds. How do you play?

Assuming trumps to break 3–2, you have four trump tricks,
one heart and a heart ruff, the ace of diamonds and the two top
clubs—nine tricks in all. The tenth could come from diamonds or
from a successful club finesse.

If the diamonds are no worse than 4–2 you will always be able
to establish the fifth diamond for a club discard—as long as you
do not release the ace of diamonds on the first round. But is there
not a danger that West's four of diamonds is a singleton? That is
so, but if West is short in diamonds he is likely to be long in clubs,
which makes the club finesse a dubious bet. Furthermore, even if
West *can* ruff a diamond return it may well be at the cost of his
natural trump trick. On balance it seems best to allow East to win
the second trick.

But be sure to avoid the careless play of the knave or the ten of
diamonds from dummy. The two is the proper card to play in
order not to waste the power of your seven.

Say East wins with the nine and returns a club. You will play
the king and draw two rounds of trumps with the king and ace.
Now a diamond towards dummy will disclose the position. If
West shows out you will still be able to establish a second diamond
trick by ruffing out East's king and queen.

A TIME FOR THINKING

♠ A
♡ A K 7 6
♦ Q 10
♣ J 10 9 8 5 2

Game all

North	South
1 ♣	1 ♦
1 ♡	2 NT
3 NT	—

♠ K Q 5
♡ 9 2
♦ K J 9 8 7
♣ Q 6 3

West leads the four of spades against your three no trump contract. Can you make sure of nine tricks?

The tricks appear to be there all right. You have five winners in the major suits and a further four tricks can be developed in either minor. The only snag is that you may have difficulty with entries.

If you first tackle the diamonds the opponents will no doubt hold up the ace until the second round and thereafter deny you access to your own hand, so it looks as though the better line of attack is to play on clubs.

At trick two you lead the knave of clubs from dummy. East, let us say, wins with the ace and returns a heart and West's ten forces a high heart from dummy. Now you are in danger of losing two hearts, a diamond and two clubs, so you must abandon the club suit for the moment and switch to diamonds. You play the queen of diamonds from dummy and overtake with your king. The opponents must hold off, otherwise you will make four diamond tricks and your contract. You make good use of the entry to your hand by cashing one high spade, discarding one of dummy's heart losers, and now a switch back to clubs ensures nine tricks.

No dazzling technique was required here, but it would be easy enough to mess up the timing if you failed to plan ahead at trick one.

♠ 5
♡ A Q 2
◇ A Q 8 7 5 3   *Game all*
♣ 8 6 4

              South   *North*

♠ Q 9 4 3   1 ♣   1 ◇
♡ K 6   3 ♣   6 ♣
◇ 4
♣ A K Q J 9 3

Against your small slam West leads the two of clubs. You play the four from dummy, East covers with the five and your nine wins. How should you continue?

On any other lead you would have been able to ruff two spades in dummy. Now you will most likely get only one spade ruff, which with six trumps, three hearts and a diamond will leave you a trick short.

The diamond finesse offers a fifty-fifty chance of making the contract of course, but you should be able to get better odds than that. By using both the ace and the queen of hearts as entries to dummy, thereby sacrificing your third heart trick, you will be able to establish two long diamond tricks if the suit breaks no worse than 4–2—an 84 per cent chance.

At trick two you will concede a spade to the defenders, winning the probable trump return and continuing with a diamond to the ace and diamond ruffed high. After a spade ruff and another diamond ruffed high you will draw the outstanding trump, if there is one, discarding the small heart from dummy. Now the king of hearts to dummy's ace and a final diamond ruff will make dummy good.

There is one further small point which could prove to be vital. The spade you lead at the second trick should be the queen. The original holding of either opponent (although more likely East on the bidding) could be ♠ A K x, ♡ x x x x, ◇ K J 9 x x, ♣ x, in which case you will be able to ruff two spades in dummy after all.

♠ J 9 3
♡ A K 8 6
♢ A K 7 6 3
♣ Q

North-South game

South	North
1 ♣	2 ♢
2 ♠	3 ♡
4 ♢	4 ♠
6 ♣	—

♠ A K Q 10
♡ 4 2
♢ Q 5
♣ A 9 7 5 4

West leads the five of trumps against your contract of six spades. How do you plan the play?

If the last lead was unfriendly this one is positively diabolical. Didn't anyone ever tell West that he shouldn't lead trumps against a small slam?

Now if you play to ruff two clubs in dummy you will have to trely on a 3–3 trump break, for your only way back to your hand ho draw trumps will be by a heart or diamond ruff. On the other hand if you allow for trumps to be 4–2 it looks as though you will have to find the diamonds 3–3, in which case you might as well have bid seven spades. Of course after ruffing one club and drawing trumps you may still get home on a 4–2 diamond break if the defender with the long diamonds is now out of clubs. Can you see anything better to go for?

In fact the contract can always be made even if both spades and diamonds break 4–2. The correct line is to play a low diamond from both hands at trick two. This duck preserves control of the situation, allowing you to cope with any return the opponents may make. If another trump comes back you can play off the ace of clubs and ruff a club with dummy's last trump, returning to your hand with the queen of diamonds to draw trumps.

♠ K J 10
♡ J 8 6
◇ Q J   *Love all*
♣ J 7 6 4 3

	South	North
	1 ◇	1 NT
♠ A Q 9 3 | 2 ♠ | 3 ♠ |
♡ 3 | 4 ♠ | — |
◇ A K 9 7 3
♣ A 8 2

West leads the king of hearts against your four spade contract, East encourages with the nine, and West continues with the four of hearts to his partner's ace. How do you plan your play?

It is a little disconcerting to find only three trumps in dummy, particularly in view of this forcing lead. To ruff and draw trumps will succeed only when the trumps break 3–3, so perhaps it would be better to discard a club loser on this trick and the other club loser if the opponents lead a third round of hearts. Now dummy would be able to take care of a fourth round of hearts, while if the defenders switch to clubs to knock out your ace you could play off the queen and knave of diamonds and then draw trumps, succeeding if neither trumps nor diamonds break worse than 4–2.

The advantages of this line of play are illusory, however. Your contract is on ice if the diamonds stand up for two rounds, even if trumps break worse than 4–2. The proper play is to ruff the second trick, lead a diamond to dummy and a diamond back to your hand. Now the quality of your trumps will enable you to make them all separately. A diamond ruff, a club to your ace, a diamond ruff, a heart ruff and another diamond ruff will leave you with two winning trumps in your hand and a total of ten tricks.

```
♠ 84
♡ A K 7 3
◇ K Q 9 7 4 2                Love all
♣ 6
                        South    North
                        1 NT     2 ♣
♠ Q 9 5 2               2 ♠      3 ◇
♡ Q 10 4                3 NT     —
◇ A 8
♣ A J 7 2
```

West leads the two of hearts against your three no trump contract. How do you plan the play?

The lead is friendly for a change, giving you a present of the fourth heart trick. With a normal diamond break you will make no fewer than eleven tricks, so you should base your plan of campaign on the assumption that diamonds will be 4–1. You need not fear four diamonds with West, for in that case you can simply concede a diamond trick. With the lead at that side of the table the opponents will be able to cash no more than three spade tricks. If East has the diamond stopper the situation is more dangerous. East might also have a spade holding such as A J 3, or K 10 6, in which case the lead of the middle honour card would pick up four spade tricks for the defence.

What you have to look for is a way of improving your prospects if East is inconsiderate enough to hold four diamonds. The solution begins to come into focus when you reflect that of the five diamond singletons West could hold two are honour cards. If West has the bare knave or ten of diamonds it will be possible to lose your diamond trick to him even though East has the real stopper. The first diamond lead will have to come from dummy, though, and that will not be possible if you allow the opening lead to run round to your hand.

The proper play is the ace or king of hearts at trick one, refusing the offer of a free heart trick. You should then lead a small diamond from dummy and, if East plays low, give yourself the best chance of nine tricks by playing the eight from your hand.

A TIME FOR THINKING

♠ A 9 6 4
♡ A 8 7 5
◇ A 4
♣ A 9 3

Game all

South	North
3 ◇	5 ◇
—	

♠ 7
♡ 9 2
◇ K Q 8 7 6 5 2
♣ K 5 4

West leads the queen of clubs against your five diamond contract. How do you plan the play?

It looks as though you may have missed it this time. Seven trumps and four outside winners add up to eleven tricks, and there is a good chance of a squeeze for the twelfth.

As always when the contract looks easy, you should ask yourself what could go wrong. Clearly nothing but a 4–0 trump break can hurt you here. Well, what can you do about it if someone is void in trumps? If it is East, nothing, but if West has no trumps there is a good chance that you will be able to make all your small trumps by *coup en passant*, so long as you take the proper precautions at an early stage.

The correct play, after winning the first trick with the king of clubs, is to lead the king of diamonds. If West shows out you will continue with a spade to the ace and a spade ruff, and then duck a heart. Say a club is returned. You will win with dummy's ace, ruff another spade, and play a heart to the ace. If all has gone well up to now you are in the clear. A heart ruff and a trump to dummy's ace followed by a spade or a heart lead from dummy will enable you to make your remaining small trump. If East ruffs in at any time you can simply discard your club loser.

Although the technique used here is that of the trump coup, the play of the king of diamonds at trick two is basically a safety measure to guard against a possible bad trump break.

29

♠ K Q
♡ —
♢ A Q 10 9 6 2
♣ Q 9 7 4 2

Game all

South	West	North	East
3 ♠	4 ♡	4 ♠	—
—	5 ♣	Double	5 ♡
5 ♠	Double	all pass	

♠ A J 9 8 6 5 4 3
♡ Q 8 3
♢ 5
♣ 6

After a lively auction West leads the ace of clubs against your doubled contract of five spades. East follows with the eight of clubs and West now switches to the ace of hearts. How do you plan the play?

Eight trumps, two heart ruffs and the ace of diamonds would give you eleven tricks, but do you really expect to be able to make all your trumps separately? If West had a trump he would surely have led it in preference to the ace of hearts, so East must have 10 7 2 in trumps, which will be worth a trick if you ruff two hearts in dummy. Since you can afford to ruff only one heart you must set up your eleventh trick in diamonds, but dummy is uncomfortably short of entries.

Think for a moment about West's hand. His distribution is likely to be 0–6–1–6 or 0–6–2–5, and if he has the top honours in both his suits you may be able to embarrass him by allowing him to hold the second trick. Unable to continue hearts or clubs without giving you the eleventh trick he will have to switch to diamonds. You will still have a guess to make in the diamond suit, of course. To finesse the queen will win when West has K x in the suit, but the more promising line is to play the ace and continue with the queen, running it if East plays low. This method will succeed when West started with J x, xx, or any singleton diamond.

The waiting move of ducking the second trick is not too obvious. It would be easy to miss at the table.

A TIME FOR THINKING

♠ 7
♡ 9 8 4 2
◇ A K Q J 6
♣ 8 6 3

Game all

South	North
1 ♠	2 ◇
3 ♡	4 ♡
4 ♠	5 ◇
6 ♣	6 ♡

♠ A K 9 6 2
♡ A K J 10 7
◇ 9 7 4
♣ —

West leads the king of clubs against your six heart contract. How do you plan the play?

The hand looks almost too easy and for that reason alone it should be treated with special care.

It is clear that your contract can be in danger only when West has all the outstanding trumps. In that event you will be unable to ruff spades in dummy, for that line of play would leave you open to a club force. For your twelve tricks you will have to play on reverse dummy lines, planning to take three trumps, two club ruffs, five diamonds and two spades. To keep control of the trump situation you will have to allow West to win the second round after East shows out.

But when you let West in he may, instead of continuing with clubs, return a third round of trumps. If you have to win this in hand you will be unable to cope with the case where West has a singleton diamond. You will be short of an entry to dummy, unable to obtain the extra ruff you need *and* draw West's remaining trump.

Catering for every eventuality requires a high degree of foresight before playing a card from your hand. You should ruff the first trick with the ten of hearts and then lay down the ace. When East shows out you continue with the knave as planned. Now if West leads a third round of trumps you can win with the eight in dummy, ruff a second club with your king, and re-enter dummy in diamonds to draw the last trump with the nine.

The distribution you have to guard against is as follows:

Oddly enough the unblocking play of ruffing the first trick with an intermediate honour would also be correct if your contract were seven hearts. The cards could be distributed like this:

If you win the first trick with the seven of trumps you can wave good-bye to the grand slam. If you ruff correctly with the ten, on the other hand, after cashing the ace of hearts and ruffing a spade in dummy you will be able to draw trumps, the last round of which will squeeze West in spades and diamonds for the thirteenth trick.

CHAPTER 2

Counting the Hand

In the play of the hand the declarer enjoys an enormous advantage over the defenders in that he knows the exact strength and disposition of the forces at his command. This knowledge enables him to bring a variety of well-defined techniques to the business of setting up his long suits, establishing his winners and limiting his losers. It follows that the ability to count the hand is relatively less important in dummy play than in defence, where knowledge is more limited, technique more obscure, and the winning line harder to spot. To the defenders counting is practically the alpha and omega of good play, while to declarer it is no more than an adjunct to technique.

Perhaps this is just as well, for on many hands it is by no means easy for declarer to discover the distribution of the opposing holdings, particularly when the defenders have taken no part in the bidding. Nevertheless, counting can play a vital role in all phases of dummy play, and it should be an integral part of the game of all players who have any aspirations. The player who makes a real effort to work out his opponents' holdings will always enjoy an overwhelming advantage over the mechanical player who sees only the twenty-six cards in front of him. It is no exaggeration to say that the ability to count the hand is in itself enough to make the difference between a losing player and a winning one.

For anyone with sufficient determination it is not really difficult to acquire this ability. The arithmetic is simple enough, involving nothing more than adding up to thirteen, but a sustained effort of concentration is required. It is necessary to keep a constant watch on the small cards played by the defenders, for if you do not notice when an opponent shows out of a suit it will obviously be impossible for you to make use of the information. You must be prepared to practise counting, not just now and then, but on every hand you play. This does not mean that you will need to get a count on every hand. On most hands the count will be of no use to you. But if you do not cultivate the habit of counting on every hand you are likely to find that you fail to get the count when you really do need it. At first this will seem like a lot of hard work with no immediate results to show for it, but the rewards of persistence are sure.

One day you will find yourself making a tricky contract by taking a deep finesse that you *know* must be right, where the week before you might unthinkingly have played for the drop. Suddenly the trick will be there. You will have acquired a new skill, like riding a bicycle or walking a tight-rope, and there will be no holding you back.

♠ 7 3
♡ K 8 6 5
◇ K Q 8 3   *Game all*
♣ K 7 2

	South	North
	1 ♡	3 ♡
	6 ♡	—

♠ A K 5
♡ A Q J 7 2
◇ A
♣ J 10 6 4

The bidding may be unscientific, but at least it is uninformative. Many of the most interesting contracts stem from bidding such as this.

West leads the knave of spades against your six heart contract. East plays the queen and you win with the ace. You draw trumps in two rounds, cash the ace of diamonds and the king of spades, and ruff your small spade in dummy. East discards the three of clubs on this trick. You play off the king and queen of diamonds and discard two clubs from your hand. When you lead the last diamond from dummy East throws the five of clubs. How should you continue?

Provided that you do a little counting and keep your wits about you, the slam is within your grasp. Try counting East's hand. He had two spades, two hearts and three diamonds, and therefore all six outstanding clubs. If you prefer to count West's hand the answer will still be the same. West has shown up with six spades, two hearts and five diamonds, which leaves room for nary a club. So all you need to do is to discard a further club on the fourth round of diamonds, allowing West to win. He will have to return a spade or a diamond, giving you a ruff and discard and your slam.

It is not always possible to achieve a perfect count of the distribution of the unseen hands as in the above deal. More often we have to rely on an inferential count. When the opponents enter the auction each bid they make tells us something about their distribution. The inferences thus obtained may enable us to draw up a blueprint of the enemy holdings sufficiently accurate for our purpose.

♠ 5 4
♡ K 9 8 3 2
♢ A J 8 7   *North-South game*
♣ A 3
                        South   *West*   *North*   *East*
                         1 ♡   2 ♣   4 ♡   —
♠ A 8 7
♡ A Q 10 6 4   —   4 ♠   5 ♡   all pass
♢ K 6 5
♣ 7 5

West leads the king of spades against your five heart contract and you play low in both hands. West now switches to the king of clubs. You win in dummy and play two rounds of trumps, East discarding a diamond on the second round. How should you continue?

As long as you remember the bidding you are not likely to go wrong here. West must surely have five spades to have bid the suit at the four-level, and he will not have fewer clubs. He has shown up with two trumps, so there is not much room for diamonds in his hand. Very likely he is void in diamonds, although he could conceivably have a singleton. But the important thing is that he cannot possibly have more than one diamond. You should therefore play the ace of spades and ruff your small spade in dummy, cash one top diamond (it doesn't matter which), and exit with your club loser. If West wins he will have to concede a ruff and discard, while if East takes the trick he will have the additional choice of leading away from his queen of diamonds.

West was unfortunate in his choice of lead. An original attack on clubs would have given you no chance worth mentioning.

♠ A 9 4 3
♡ A 7
♢ A 9 6 5 2   *Game all*
♣ 7 5

	West	North	East	South
♠ K Q J 8 2	3 ♡	—	4 ♡	4 ♠
♡ 4	—	4 NT	—	6 ♣
♢ 8 3	—	6 ♠	all pass	
♣ A K Q 10 4				

West leads the king of hearts against your spade slam and you win with dummy's ace. East discards hearts on the second and third round of trumps. On the ace of clubs West plays the eight and East the two. How should you continue?

For his vulnerable three-bid West must surely have started with seven hearts. He followed to three rounds of spades, so can have only three cards in the minors. It may be that you have to finesse the ten of clubs on the second round, but you would feel foolish if you lost to a doubleton knave.

The way to find out if the finesse is necessary or not is to duck a round of diamonds. If a diamond is returned you will have an exact count of West's hand. Should he follow to the second round of diamonds you can finesse the ten of clubs with complete confidence, while if he discards on the second diamond you will know that the clubs can be established without finessing.

If West wins the first diamond and returns a heart, you will follow the same line of play, ruffing and playing a diamond to the ace to obtain the count.

The only variation in which you are denied an immediate count is where East wins the diamond and returns a club. Fortunately there is now an alternative line of play to ensure the contract. You play off the top clubs and ruff the fourth round in dummy. A heart ruff in your hand is followed by your last trump and East, if he began with five clubs, is now squeezed in clubs and diamonds.

♠ 8 4
♡ K 9 4 3
◇ A 8 6   *Game all*
♣ K 10 7 2

	West	North	East	South
	—	—	1 ♠	3 ♡
	4 ♠	6 ♡	all pass	

♠ 10
♡ A Q J 10 8 5
◇ K 4
♣ A 9 6 4

West leads the two of spades against your six heart contract.
East wins with the king and continues with the ace of spades. You
ruff and draw trumps, East discarding a spade on the second
round. What now?

You wish your partner had been a little less exuberant, for you
will need a large slice of luck to bring home this slam. One
opponent must have either a singleton honour or queen-jack bare
in clubs to give you a chance.

As always, the correct method is to find out as much as possible
about the enemy distribution before tackling the critical suit. Three
rounds of diamonds may bring some enlightenment. Suppose, for
instance, that East discards a spade on the third round of diamonds. Now you know all. If the opening lead was honest West
is marked with four spades, he has shown up with two hearts and
six diamonds, and therefore has a singleton club. You must try a
small club to the king in the hope that West's singleton is an
honour.

If both opponents follow to three rounds of diamonds the
position may still be obscure, but at least you know that East cannot have four clubs. You therefore cash the ace of clubs first. If
East drops an honour you will have to guess well on the second
round.

It happens occasionally that the bidding and the play to the
first few tricks will enable you to place every card in your opponents' hands at an early stage.

♠ K 6 5
♡ A K
◇ K Q 7 2   *Love all*
♣ 10 9 8 3

	West	North	East	South
	—	—	1 ◇	1 ♠
♠ A Q 9 7 4 3	2 ◇	4 ♠	all pass	
♡ J 10 7 5 4				
◇ 8 5				
♣ —				

Against your four spade contract West leads the knave of diamonds, which is covered by dummy's queen and East's ace. East
now tries to cash the ace of clubs but you ruff and play on hearts.
To your annoyance East ruffs the second round of hearts and
returns a diamond to his partner's ten and dummy's king. How do
you continue?

To make your contract you will need to get a heart ruff in
dummy. It seems not unreasonable to hope to draw the three outstanding trumps with the king and ace before doing so, but a
pause for reflection on the bidding will convince you that this line
of play cannot succeed. Since West supported his partner's diamonds East must have opened with a four-card suit. He had only
one heart, and therefore must have started with eight cards in the
black suits. But with a good five card club suit East would surely
have bid it in preference to his anaemic diamonds. It follows that
East's distribution must have been 4–1–4–4, and West is therefore
void in spades.

It is a lot easier to play well when you know the exact enemy
holdings. If East does not split his honours on the lead of a small
trump from the table you will finesse the nine, earning admiring
(or suspicious) gasps from the kibitzers. You will then ruff your
small heart with dummy's king of spades, draw the remaining
trumps and concede a trick to the queen of hearts.

♠ A K 7 4
♡ A K Q 6 5
◇ J   *Game all*
♣ 9 8 7

	West	North	East	South
	—	1 ♡	2 ♣	2 ◇
♠ 8 6 2	—	2 ♠	3 ♣	3 NT
♡ 10 7	all pass			
◇ K 8 7 6 4 3				
♣ A K				

West leads the ten of clubs against your three no trump contract. At trick two you lead the seven of hearts, on which West plays the two, dummy the ace, and East, annoyingly, the two of diamonds. On dummy's knave of diamonds East plays the ace, returning the queen of clubs on which West discards the three of hearts. The king of diamonds now produces the ten from West, you throw the club from dummy, and East follows with the nine. How do you continue?

The ninth trick will have to be obtained from spades or hearts. If the spades are 3–3 your only hope is that West holds Q J x, or that he has Q x x and fails to spot the need to unblock on the second round. But both the bidding and the play to date make it appear more likely that the spades will break 4–2. East would have to be a brave man to venture to the three-level when vulnerable with a holding of ♠ 10 x x, ♡ —, ◇ A 9 x, ♣ Q J x x x x x. Also, with that holding he would be most unlikely to discard a diamond on the first round of hearts.

So West will have four spades, which makes your task rather easier. You lead the ten of hearts which West must cover, and dummy wins. Now the ace, king, and a third round of spades puts West on lead, and he will have to allow dummy to make two more heart tricks in the end game.

When this hand turned up in a six-table masters individual event five of the South players failed to make three no trumps.

♠ 9 6 5
♡ Q 8 5 2
◇ 9 8 3   *Love all*
♣ A Q 6

South	West	North	East
1 ♡	—	2 ♡	2 ♠
4 ♡	all pass		

♠ Q 4
♡ A K J 10 6
◇ A K Q
♣ 9 8 4

West dutifully leads the ten of spades against your four heart contract. East cashes the king and ace and continues with a third round of spades, which you ruff high while West discards a diamond. It takes three rounds to draw the trumps, East following and West throwing a club and a diamond. Now you play off the ace and king of diamonds and both opponents follow. How should you continue?

This is not too difficult a problem if you have done your chores and counted East's hand. He has showed up with six spades, three hearts and two diamonds, and so cannot have more than two clubs. That means that you can make your contract for certain. A club to the ace is followed by a diamond back to your queen and then another club. If West plays low you put up dummy's queen, and if East can win this trick he will have to concede a ruff and discard.

Had East discarded on the second round of diamonds you would know he had three clubs. You could no longer be certain of making the contract although there would still be a good chance. You would have to try for a different end-play by cashing the queen of diamonds and running the nine of clubs, playing dummy's queen only if West covered. If East's king captured the queen, on the forced club return you would have to guess whether East's concealed club was the seven or the remaining honour card.

♠ Q J 7
♡ 10 4
◇ K 8 6 5
♣ 8 7 4 3

Game all

South	*North*
2 ♣	2 ◇
2 NT	3 NT
—	

♠ A 10 5
♡ A 7 6 2
◇ A Q J
♣ A K Q

West leads the king of hearts against your contract of three no trumps. You let him win this trick, and when he continues with the queen of hearts you hold off again. On the third round of hearts you throw a spade from dummy in order to retain all the chances in the minor suits. East discards a diamond on this trick and you win with the ace. You play off the three top clubs and East discards a spade on the third round. Now you try the diamonds, leading the ace followed by the queen. West discards a spade on the second round. How should you continue?

By now you have a count of West's hand and your contract is unbeatable provided that you keep track of what is going on. West started with three spades, five hearts, one diamond and four clubs. At the moment he has left in his hand two spades, two winning hearts and a winning club.

The lead of the knave of diamonds will squeeze West in three suits. If he throws the master club you can overtake with the diamond king and cash dummy's club. If he throws a heart you will play low in dummy and put him on lead with your last heart. After making his club trick he will have to lead spades into your major tenace. Finally, if he throws a spade you will again play low in dummy and continue with the ace and another spade. If the king does not fall under your ace East must have it, and he will have to return a spade or a diamond to give you your ninth trick.

♠ K 7
♡ K 10 8 5 2
◇ J 8 6 5 3   *Game all*
♣ 4

♠ —   *West*   *North*   *East*   *South*
♡ A Q J 9 4 3   3 ♠   —   4 ♠   5 ♡
◇ A 7 2   all pass
♣ K Q J 7

West leads the queen of spades against your five heart contract, East plays the ace on dummy's king and you ruff. Both opponents follow when you lead a heart to the king, and on the club return West captures your king with his ace. He returns the knave of spades which you ruff. What now?

West should have seven spades for his vulnerable three-bid; with eight he might have opened four or contested further. That gives West five cards in the minors and East eight. There is no real chance of a squeeze on East, for if you duck a diamond the enemy are sure to return the suit, removing your entry. It is better to hope for some kind of blockage in diamonds.

Is there anything to be said for playing the diamond ace immediately? Something, but not a great deal. The play would have a dubious chance of gain if West has K 9, Q 9, K 4, or Q 4 in diamonds and fails to spot the need to unblock. But it would give up all hope when West has a singleton diamond.

It is best to play off the clubs and try to get an accurate count. Suppose both opponents follow to four rounds of clubs. Now you know that West has a singleton diamond and your next play should be a small diamond from both hands, hoping that West's singleton is the king, queen or ten. If West proves to have two or three clubs you will know that the diamonds are breaking 3–2. After ruffing the last club you will play the ace and another diamond in the hope that a blockage exists.

Finally, if West proves to have a singleton club and four diamonds, there are two sure ways of making the contract. I leave it to you to work them out.

♠ 6 3
♡ Q 7 4 3
◇ K 5   *North-South game*
♣ Q 8 6 5 2

West	North	East	South
4 ♡	—	—	4 ♠
all pass			

♠ A K J 10 8
♡ 8
◇ A Q 6
♣ A 10 9 4

As you will realize, it is easier to count the hand when there are long suits about, hence the high proportion of pre-emptive bids in this chapter.

West starts off with the ace of hearts on which his partner drops the king. The knave of hearts is continued and you play low from dummy, but East ruffs with the nine of spades anyway and you over-ruff. You play trumps from the top, West's queen winning the third round while East discards a diamond. West plugs away with the ten of hearts. How do you play to make sure of your contract?

West had seven hearts and three spades, therefore only three cards in the minor suits. Once again the way to find out how to tackle clubs is to test the diamonds first. But there is a further trap in this hand. The only completely safe method of play is to refuse once again to put up the queen of hearts, ruffing instead with your last trump. Now the play of the ace of diamonds followed by the small diamond to the king will clear up the situation.

If West shows out on the first or second round of diamonds, a club to the ace and a club back towards the queen will ensure ten tricks. But if West follows to two rounds of diamonds you can afford to try for an overtrick by leading the club queen from dummy, hoping to pin the knave in West's hand. Should West's singleton happen to be the king instead, he will have to put you back in dummy to take the proven finesse against the knave.

♠ 8 4
♡ K Q 9 3
◇ Q
♣ K J 7 5 4 3   *North-South game*

♠ K 6 3   *South*   *West*   *North*   *East*
♡ A 10 8 6 4   1 ♡   3 ♠   4 ♡   all pass
◇ A K 5
♣ Q 9

Against your four heart contract West leads the eight of clubs
to his partner's ace. East returns the knave of spades, you play
low, and West overtakes with the queen. He continues with the
ace of spades, his partner discarding a diamond, and then the ten
of spades. You ruff high in dummy and East discards another
diamond. How should you continue?

The problem is how to handle trumps. Should you play for the
drop of the knave or take a second round finesse? Which way
would you finesse anyway? Or would it be safe to play on the side
suits in order to find out how the trumps lie?

Think for a moment about the club position. West's eight cannot have been a singleton or he would not have overtaken the
spade knave. East would also know the position and would have
ruffed the ace of spades to lead a club back if he started with four
of them. Nor can West have had three clubs originally, for then
East would have discarded his second club on the ace of spades in
order to get a ruff. West must have started with two clubs and
therefore four cards in the red suits, and the indications are that
he is not void in diamonds.

Your proper play is to cash the queen of diamonds, return to
hand with the queen of clubs, and count out West's hand by
continuing with diamonds.

Note that East could have made your task more difficult by
discarding his clubs on the second and third rounds of spades.

♠ A 7 6 2
♡ K Q 9 6 4
◇ 10 4
♣ A 3

Game all

	South	West	North	East
	1 ♡	—	2 ♠	3 ◇
	3 ♠	—	4 ♣	—
	4 ◇	—	4 ♡	—
	5 ♣	—	6 ♡	all pass

♠ Q 8 5 4
♡ A J 10 8 3
◇ —
♣ K J 7 5

West leads the five of diamonds against your six heart contract, and you regard dummy with mixed emotions. Your partner's rather eccentric bidding might have landed you in a spade contract at a dangerously high level. All has turned out well, however. Six hearts must have an excellent chance of success, since the king of spades is likely to be with East on the bidding.

You ruff East's ace of diamonds and draw the outstanding trumps in two rounds, East following twice while West discards a diamond. Now you test the clubs by playing ace, king and another. Surprisingly, West plays the queen on the third round and you ruff in dummy. How should you continue?

If you have been counting you will realize that the picture has altered considerably. East would not make a vulnerable bid at the three-level without at least six cards in his suit, but he also had two hearts and apparently four clubs. He can have at the most one spade, which makes it unlikely that you will be able to establish your queen of spades by leading towards it.

Fortunately you have a simple elimination play to fall back on. You should ruff dummy's last diamond and cash the knave of clubs, discarding a spade from dummy. Now a small spade from both hands will put the opponents on the spot. If West wins he will have the choice of leading a spade away from his king or leading a diamond to give you a ruff and discard. If East takes the trick he will have nothing to return but diamonds.

♠ 10 9 4
♡ 8 6 3   *Game all*
◇ K Q 7 6
♣ A K Q

	South	North
	1 ♠	2 ◇
♠ K Q J 8 2	2 ♡	3 NT
♡ A Q 7 4	4 ◇	4 ♠
◇ A 9 3	4 NT	5 ◇
♣ 8	6 ♠	—

West leads the knave of clubs against your six spade contract. You tackle the trumps and East discards a heart on the second round. On the next round East throws a club, while West takes his ace and plays a second club to dummy. You come to hand with the ace of diamonds and draw the outstanding trump, dummy and East discarding hearts. How should you continue?

Your slam has several chances of success. The diamonds might break evenly, the heart king could be with East, and there is always the possibility of a heart-diamond squeeze against either opponent. To squeeze technicians it will be obvious that you must play off your last trump, discarding another heart from dummy, before testing the diamonds. This is the proper technique even if there is no conceivable squeeze in the offing. Long trumps should not be allowed to stagnate in your hand. Whenever it can do no harm you should play them out, forcing discards from the opponents, for this may make it easier for you to count the hand.

In the present deal East's hand might be something like ♠ x, ♡ J 10 9 x x, ◇ J 10 x x, ♣ x x x. In that case your last trump will force him to part with a third heart. Then you test the diamonds and find that they do not break. But dummy's third club squeezes East out of his fourth heart. When you lead a heart from the table at trick twelve and East plays the knave you know that his last card is a diamond, so you play your ace and make the contract in spectacular fashion by dropping West's king.

47

♠ K 7 2
♡ 9 8 5
◇ J 8 3
♣ A 9 6 5

Game all

	South	North
	1 ♡	1 NT
	2 ♠	4 ♡

♠ A Q 6 4
♡ K Q J 10 4
◇ K Q 2
♣ 3

West leads the ten of diamonds against your four heart contract. East wins with the ace and shoots back the four. You win in hand and try to slip through the queen of hearts, but West goes up with the ace and leads a third diamond which his partner ruffs. East now leads the knave of spades. You win with the ace and cash the king of hearts, on which East discards a club. How should you continue?

There will be no difficulty if the spades break evenly, but what if they are 4–2? Will it be possible to ruff your fourth spade with dummy's last trump?

You know that West started with five diamonds and three trumps. If he had four spades that would leave him with only one club which he might well have led originally. Also, East would probably have entered the bidding if he had seven clubs and the ace of diamonds. Thus if either opponent has four spades it is likely to be East, in which case the only hope is to squeeze him in the black suits.

The proper play is to lead a club to the ace, ruff a club in hand with a high trump, and then lead your four of hearts to dummy's nine. If East's original distribution was 4–2–2–5 he will be squeezed on this trick. He will either have to unguard the spades or throw his penultimate club, which will allow you to ruff out his remaining club and establish dummy's nine as a winner.

♠ Q 4
♡ K J 9 4
◊ 9 8 2
♣ 8 6 5 3

East-West game

South	North
1 ♡	2 ♡
2 NT	3 ♡
—	

♠ A J 8
♡ A Q 10 2
◊ A 5 4
♣ Q 7 4

West leads the ace of clubs against your three heart contract. East encourages with the knave and West continues with the two of clubs to his partner's king, ruffing your queen on the third round. West now switches to a trump. How do you plan the play?

Your chances of making this contract are not very bright. The only hope of avoiding two diamond losers is that the opponents will have communication trouble in the suit. You will have to find one defender with either a high doubleton or a singleton in diamonds. Also, West will need to have started with exactly three trumps and East two, for after drawing trumps and ruffing a spade you will need a trump left in dummy if any elimination play is to work. That gives West eight cards in spades and diamonds to East's seven. It is too early to tell who is short in diamonds, but three rounds of spades may shed some light on the matter.

It goes without saying that you need the spade finesse to be right as well, and it must be correct to win the first trump in dummy and lead the queen of spades straight away to resolve the position. This will save you from going more than one down if the spade finesse is wrong. But suppose East covers the queen of spades with the king and your ace wins. Now the proper sequence of play is a heart to dummy, a diamond to the ace, then the knave of spades and a spade ruff.

If both opponents follow to the third round of spades you will know that only East can have a doubleton diamond. You will ruff dummy's last club and then lead a diamond in the hope that East's diamonds were K Q (or that he has failed to unblock from K x).

If East shows out on the third spade West is marked with the doubleton diamond. Now it would be a mistake to ruff dummy's club, for that would give West the chance to get rid of the blocking diamond. You simply play a diamond from the table instead.

A third variation arises when West shows out on the third round of spades. The count now shows that East began with a singleton diamond (presumably it was the queen since West refused to lead the suit). In this case the winning play is to lead the club from dummy and allow East to hold the trick, discarding a diamond from your hand.

CHAPTER 3

Card-Placing

In the last chapter we practised drawing inferences from the defenders' bids, leads and discards in order to discover how the suits were distributed in the enemy hands. We are going to continue to explore the opponents' holdings, but in this chapter we shall concern ourselves with high cards rather than distribution. In other words we shall count points instead of suit-lengths.

Many players do not make full use of the information available to them in planning the play of the hand. After making a hash of a delicate hand a declarer will often be heard to complain that there was nothing to guide him to the winning line. Usually the truth is that he has not seen what was under his nose. While play is in progress the air around the bridge table is positively vibrating with inferences of every kind. All you have to do is to tune in to the right frequency to pick them up.

Every time an opponent bids or doubles he is offering you a slice of free information which it would be foolish to disregard. All aspects of the enemy behaviour should be kept in mind for handy reference during the play. The choice of suit for the opening lead has its own story to tell. So has the card selected, the card played in following suit, the choice of discard, and the general direction of the attack. Just as important are the negative inferences which can be drawn when an opponent fails to bid or double, fails to lead trumps, fails to hold up a stopper or fails to adopt an obvious line of defence.

Inferences come in all shapes and sizes. Some are subtle and hard to define while others are so blatant that they seem to shriek at you. Some inferences are more fallible than others. Many are valid in all circumstances, but occasionally the worth of an inference will depend on your estimate of the skill of the defenders.

At times you will find that the evidence before you is incomplete, that you have insufficient data upon which to base a firm conclusion. Then, as in the previous chapter, you must try to plan the play so as to discover as much as possible about the location of the cards before tackling the critical suit.

The ideal will not always be attainable. There will be occasions when, for one reason or another, you cannot afford to mess about and discover as much as you would like before taking action. In such cases you will have to fall back on your imagination. If you are worried about the possibility of a certain opponent holding one of the missing key cards, assume that he has it and picture to yourself what his hand will then look like. Relating this imaginary hand to the bidding (or lack of bidding, as the case may be) will often enable you to draw helpful conclusions about the position of missing honour cards.

♠ J 9 6 3
♡ A 10 7 5 3
♢ 10 9 4
♣ J

	West	North	East	South
	1 ♢	—	—	2 ♠
	3 ♢	3 ♠	—	4 ♠
	all pass			

North-South game

♠ A Q 10 8 5 2
♡ Q 9
♢ 6
♣ K Q 4 2

West starts with two top diamonds against your contract of four spades. You ruff the second round and lead a club to dummy's knave. East wins and returns the eight of hearts, on which you play the nine, West the knave, and dummy the ace. How should you continue?

Since you have a loser in each of the side suits the problem is to avoid losing a trump trick. Other things being equal, the percentage play is to lead the knave of spades from dummy and run it if East plays low. But if you cast your mind back to the bidding you will realize that other things are far from equal in this case.

Although he was not strong enough to keep the bidding alive after his partner had opened with one diamond, East has already produced the ace of clubs. It is not reasonable to expect him to have the king of spades as well. With seven points he would hardly have passed his partner's opening bid.

Your only chance is to play the ace of trumps on the first round in the hope that West's hand is something like ♠ K, ♡ K J x x, ♢ A K Q J x x, ♣ x x.

The ability to drop singleton kings has long been regarded as one of the hallmarks of the expert card player, but in this hand nothing more difficult than counting up to seven is involved.

The next hand, while it is of similar type, introduces a slight variation.

♠ Q 7 2				
♡ 8 6 4 3		North-South game		
◇ K Q 7 6 5				
♣ Q	West	North	East	South
	1 ♡	—	—	Double
♠ A J 10 8 5 4	—	2 ◇	—	2 ♠
♡ Q 5 2	—	3 ♠	—	4 ♠
◇ —	all pass			
♣ A K J 6				

West leads the ace of hearts against your four spade contract and East follows with the ten. West continues with the king of hearts, East discarding the two of clubs, and a third heart which East ruffs with the three of spades. The four of clubs comes back and you allow the trick to go to dummy's queen. What do you do next?

Once again the normal method of play would be to take an immediate trump finesse, and this time there is no evidence to suggest that the finesse will fail. Just the same, there is no excuse for failing to try to dig up such evidence.

Try leading the king of diamonds from dummy. If East should by any chance have the ace he will need second sight to refrain from playing it. If he does produce the ace that is all the evidence you need. As in the previous hand, East would not have passed his partner's opening bid with seven points in his hand, so the king of spades is marked with West and you must pray that it drops under the ace.

If East plays unhesitatingly low on the king of diamonds, you will put on a trump and re-enter dummy by ruffing a club in order to take the spade finesse. There can be no danger in this line of play, for East can hardly have started with a doubleton club.

CARD-PLACING

One final variation before we leave this seven-point theme.

```
♠ A 6
♡ A Q 10 4
♦ K Q J 3
♣ 10 6 3
```

				Love all
	West	North	East	South
	—	—	1 ♠	—
♠ K 8 4	—	Double	—	2 ♡
♡ J 9 7 5 2	—	3 ♡	—	4 ♡
♦ 9 8 5	all pass			
♣ K 7				

West leads the seven of spades against your four heart contract. How do you plan the play?

The contract is certainly sound enough. The only danger is that you might lose a trump, a diamond and two clubs. Once again there is no evidence to suggest that the trump finesse will fail, and this time there is no safe way of trying to discover if such evidence exists. It would not be altogether safe to play on clubs before trumps, for instance, for that might give East the opportunity to obtain a diamond ruff if his hand is something like ♠ Q J 10 9 x, ♡ K x x, ♦ x x, ♣ A Q J.

But in this case all you need do is imagine the evidence. You know that West would not pass his partner's opening bid if he had seven points. In the dangerous case where West holds the ace of clubs, therefore, he cannot also have the king of hearts, so you might as well play the ace of hearts on the first round.

To put it another way, if the heart finesse is working there is no need for you to take it for then the ace of clubs will certainly be with East.

So you win the first trick with the ace of spades and continue with ace and another heart. If East drops the king under your ace . . . bingo!

♠ A 4 3 2
♡ Q 6 3
◇ Q 6 4 3　　　　　　*Game all*
♣ Q 6

	West	North	East	South
	—	—	1 ◇	1 ♠
♠ J 10 9 7 6 5	2 ◇	2 ♠	—	4 ♠
♡ A 8 5 4 2	all pass			
◇ 8				
♣ A				

West leads the knave of diamonds against your four spade contract and you cover with dummy's queen. East wins with the king and continues with the ace of diamonds which you ruff. On your lead of the knave of spades West plays the queen, dummy the ace and East the eight. How should you continue?

You have already lost a diamond trick and there is a certain loser in trumps, so your problem boils down to avoiding the loss of two tricks in hearts. It would be a great help if you could locate the king of hearts, for you would be able to tackle the suit with greater confidence. East has shown up with the ace and king of diamonds, and you know from the bidding that he is likely to have two of the other three kings. You will find out about the king of spades in due course, but meanwhile you must make good use of your only entry to dummy in order to find out who has the king of clubs.

The way to do that is to lead the queen of clubs from the table. If East fails to cover the queen it can fairly safely be inferred that he does not have the king. The lead of a trump from hand will now complete the picture. Should East show up with both black kings you will assume that West has the king of hearts and play accordingly. Should West prove to have either the king of clubs or the king of spades, however, the heart king must surely be with East and your only chance will be that it is only once guarded.

CARD-PLACING

♠ A 10 7 3
♡ J 6 5 2
◇ 10 8 5
♣ J 6

Love all

West	North	East	South
—	—	—	1 ♠
—	2 ♠	—	4 ♠
all pass			

♠ Q J 9 8 6 4
♡ A Q 10
◇ A
♣ K 8 7

West leads the king of diamonds against your four spade contract. How do you plan the play?

Before making up your mind how to tackle the hand you will be gathering up the threads of available evidence. From the bidding you know only that neither opponent could open or make an overcall. West presumably has the queen of diamonds to back up his king, and your contract is in danger only if he has the king of hearts and the ace of clubs as well. With all those honour cards he cannot possibly also have the king of spades or he would certainly have made himself heard during the bidding.

The correct play at trick two is therefore a spade to the ace, secure in the knowledge that if West has the king your contract is in no danger. This gives you the extra chance of dropping a singleton king in East's hand.

But suppose both opponents follow small to the ace of spades and East wins the second round with the king and returns the three of clubs. What should you do now?

The argument, although weaker, is still valid. With the king of hearts, king and queen of diamonds and the ace of clubs, West might have scraped up an opening bid or an overcall, so you should play the king of clubs on this trick. If the king is captured by the ace and you have to lose two club tricks, there is an excellent chance that the heart finesse will work.

This arbitrary placement of the opponents' key cards can often be of great value in working out a logical line of play.

♠ 10 2
♡ K J 6 5
◇ K J 7
♣ K 6 4 3   *Love all*

♠ K J 4   *South*   *West*   *North*   *East*
♡ A Q 10 8 7 3   1 ♡   —   3 ♡   all pass
◇ 6 4
♣ 8 5

West leads the six of spades against your three heart contract.
East wins with the ace and returns the eight, on which you play
the king. Your knave of spades is covered by West's queen, you
ruff high in dummy and East follows with the three. You continue
with the king of hearts and a heart to your ace, West discarding a
spade. Now what?

You need to make just one trick in the minor suits, but there is
no certain way of doing it. There is nothing you can do about the
club position—either dummy's king wins or it doesn't, but in
diamonds you have a guess to make.

If you had been more sanguine in the bidding and pushed on to
four hearts your problem would be easier in a way. Having to find
the club ace with West you would place the diamond ace with
East, for with two aces and a five card spade suit headed by the
queen West might have ventured an overcall.

But you are in three hearts and can afford the ace of clubs to be
wrong as long as you can make a diamond trick. Assume it is
wrong, then. If East has the ace of clubs he is rather less likely to
have the third ace as well, so you should plan to put up the king
of diamonds if West plays low.

On a point of technique you should, of course, tackle the diamonds first. If East *has* been kept out of the bidding on a three-
ace hand you will still make your contract if his holding is something like ♠ A 8 3, ♡ 9 4, ◇ A Q 5 3, ♣ A 10 7 4.

♠ 9 6 5 3
♡ 7 5
◇ 7 5 4 3   *East-West game*
♣ A K 10

West	North	East	South
—	—	—	1 ♠
—	2 ♠	—	2 NT
—	4 ♠	all pass	

♠ K Q 8 4
♡ Q 8
◇ A Q J 2
♣ Q J 5

West leads the nine of hearts against your four spade contract. East wins with the king and returns the six of clubs. How do you plan the play?

The annoying duplication of values means that your high cards are not pulling their full weight, and your prospects are not very bright. There is no way of avoiding a second heart loser, so it looks as though both the ace of spades and the king of diamonds will need to be with East to give you a chance of success.

But is that possible in view of the bidding? East passed originally, remember, and he appears to have both ace and king of hearts. He simply cannot have the ace of spades and the king of diamonds as well, although he might conceivably have one of those cards.

A singleton king of diamonds in West's hand will be no use to you here. If you are to make this contract it is essential that diamonds break 3–2 and that East has the king. You must therefore play on the assumption that the ace of spades is in West's hand.

After winning the second trick with dummy's ten of clubs you should lead the three of spades and, if East plays low, put in your eight, in the hope that East's hand is something like ♠ J 10 x, ♡ A K 10 x, ◇ K x x, ♣ x x x.

```
♠ K 7 4
♡ 3
◇ Q J 6 5 2                North-South game
♣ A 10 7 3
                   West    North    East    South
                    —        —       —       1 ♣
♠ Q J 6 2
♡ A K 8             —      3 ♣      —      3 NT
◇ K 8              all pass
♣ Q J 5 4
```

West leads the ten of spades against your three no trump contract. You play low in dummy and East takes the ace and switches to the four of hearts. How do you plan the play?

Counting your tricks, you see that you have six on top with possibilities of developing enough for your contract in either diamonds or clubs. It is a hand on which you might well make eleven tricks, but there is a chance that you will be held to eight. Since there is danger only when the club finesse is wrong and the diamonds fail to break, you should concentrate on that case and try to find a safe way of making nine tricks.

Assume that East has the king of clubs. He has already produced the ace of spades and presumably has a heart honour, so it becomes rather unlikely that he will also have the ace of diamonds. With a heart suit and twelve points he would probably have made a third-in-hand opening bid.

Thus in the dangerous case it is West who will have the ace of diamonds. At trick three you should therefore lead the eight of diamonds through West. If he goes up with the ace that will establish at least three diamond tricks for you, bringing your total to nine. If West plays low and dummy wins a diamond trick you will make sure of your contract by playing the ace and another club.

Should East turn up with the ace of diamonds and lead another heart you can be fairly sure that the club finesse will succeed, allowing you to make two overtricks.

CARD-PLACING

♠ A
♡ Q 9
◇ A Q 10 8 7 6 3   *East-West game*
♣ 10 8 7

North	South
1 ◇	2 ♣

♠ 9 8 3
♡ A 10
◇ 5 4
♣ A K 9 6 4 2

North	South
3 ◇	4 ♣
4 NT	5 ♡
6 ♣	—

Over-optimistic bidding and not too happy a contract—just the sort of thing that is liable to happen when you face a stranger at the rubber bridge table.

West leads the five of spades against your small slam and East encourages with the ten. You lead the ten of clubs to your ace, East playing the three and West the knave. On the lead of the five of diamonds West plays the two, you finesse dummy's queen and East drops the knave. You return the eight of clubs from dummy and East plays the five. How do you play to this trick?

According to the Principle of Restricted Choice the finesse is almost twice as likely to succeed as the play for the drop, which makes it rather hard to see that the finesse would be the wrong play here. The point is that the finesse gains nothing even if it works. If East's knave of diamonds was an honest card you are always going to make this contract by taking a second diamond finesse. The only case in which your trump view might make a difference is when East has made a deceptive play in diamonds holding K J or K J 9. If that is his holding you are not going to make the contract unless the trumps are 2–2.

The danger in taking a losing trump finesse is that West is sure to return a spade. Then you would have to return to hand with the ace of hearts and stake all on the diamonds.

If you play the king of trumps on the second round and West shows out, and you then take a losing diamond finesse you will go down, certainly, but you would have gone down even if you had finessed in trumps.

61

CARD-PLACING

♠ K 8 6
♡ A 7 2
◇ 10 3 2
♣ K 9 6 3

North-South game

West	North	East	South
—	—	1 NT*	2 ♠
—	3 ♣	—	4 ♠

all pass

♠ Q J 10 7 4
♡ Q J
◇ K
♣ A J 7 5 2

12–14 points

West leads the ten of hearts against your four spade contract. You play low in dummy and East's king wins the trick. East cashes the ace of diamonds and continues with the five of diamonds, which you ruff while West completes an echo. East wins the second round of trumps and leads the eight of diamonds to force you again. You cash the queen of hearts and lead your last trump to dummy's king, West discarding a diamond. Both opponents follow to the ace of hearts, and when you play off the king of clubs East drops the four and West the ten. You continue with a small club and East produces the eight. Do you finesse or not?

So far you have seen eleven of the points that East should have to justify his opening bid. Both opponents have played well in concealing their holdings from you as far as possible. Unless East is very cunning he is unlikely to have both queen and knave of diamonds, but he probably has one of them. His hand could be something like ♠ A x x, ♡ K x x x, ◇ A Q x x, ♣ x x, or he could equally well have ♠ A x x, ♡ K x x, ◇ A J x x, ♣ Q x x. There does not seem to be any firm conclusion to be drawn from the bidding.

But what about the play, particularly the opening lead? There is a strong negative inference available. With a weak hand would not West have led a singleton if he had one? It seems likely that he would, and you should therefore refuse the club finesse and play your ace.

CARD-PLACING

♠ A 6
♡ 9 7 4
◇ Q J 7 3
♣ K 8 5 4

Love all

♠ J 8 3
♡ Q 6 5
◇ A 6 2
♣ A Q 10 6

South	West	North	East
1 NT	all pass		

West leads the two of spades against your one no trump contract. You hopefully try the six from dummy, but East wins with the queen and returns the four of spades to dummy's ace. If the king of diamonds is wrong the opponents are likely to make too many tricks, but there is no way of avoiding the finesse so you lead the queen of diamonds from dummy at trick three. East obligingly covers with the king and your ace wins. How should you continue?

Your seven tricks are now in sight provided that you can bring in the club suit. This should be easy enough unless West has four clubs headed by the knave. Even then you have the chance that East's singleton will be the nine, creating a finessing position against West. But if you play off the ace of clubs and East drops the nine, how can you be sure it is a singleton? Holding J 9 x x, it is standard play for East to drop the nine under your ace in order to offer you an alternative to the winning line. You would feel pretty sick if you continued with the queen of clubs and West showed out.

The way to be sure of getting an honest card from East is to make him play ahead of his partner. You should return to dummy with the knave of diamonds and lead a small club from the table. It will not be safe for East to drop the nine from J 9 x x now, since for all he knows his partner may have a singleton ten in the suit. If East does produce the nine, therefore, it should be safe for you to play the queen on the second round.

♠ J 10 3
♡ K Q 7 5
♢ A K 4 3   *Game all*
♣ 10 8

	South	West	North	East
	1 ♠	2 ♣	2 ♢	—
♠ A K 8 7 2	2 ♠	—	4 ♠	all pass
♡ 6 3				
♢ Q J 6				
♣ K 7 2				

Against your four spade contract West leads the knave of hearts, covered by dummy's queen and East's ace. East returns the nine of clubs, you play small from hand, and West wins with the knave. West now switches back to the ten of hearts and dummy's king wins. How should you continue?

The only problem is to avoid losing a trump trick, and with this combination the correct percentage play is to finesse on the first round in order to guard against a holding of Q 9 x x with East. Percentages should be your servant and not your master, however. They should be called upon to determine the best line of play only when there are no other indications.

In this case there is something a little odd about the early play. West made a vulnerable overcall at the two-level and yet it was East who produced the ace of hearts. With very little outside strength West must surely have started with six cards in his suit. Why, then, did he not continue with the ace of clubs and a third round in the hope that his partner could over-ruff dummy? The answer almost certainly is that West knew quite well that his partner would be unable to over-ruff dummy, and he could only know that if the queen of spades was staring at him from his own hand.

On this reasoning you should reject the spade finesse, playing out the ace and king instead and hoping to drop the queen from West.

CARD-PLACING

♠ Q 9 6 4
♡ 8 5
◇ 10 6 3 2
♣ 10 7 2

Love all

♠ K 8 7
♡ A 7 3
◇ A J
♣ A K J 9 4

South	West	North	East
2 NT	all pass		

West leads the king of hearts against your contract of two no trumps. You let him keep this trick, and when he continues with the queen of hearts you again hold off. On the knave of hearts you throw a spade from dummy and East still follows suit. You cash the ace of clubs but nothing exciting happens, so you try the king of spades. East wins with the ace and returns the five of diamonds. Take it from there.

You have already lost three tricks and West may have two good hearts to cash when he gets in, so you must play the ace of diamonds on this trick.

In order to make your contract you must find the queen of clubs. Once again the percentage play is to cross to dummy with the queen of spades and take the club finesse. Mathematically this is almost twice as good as the alternative line of trying to drop a doubleton queen.

Nevertheless, if your inference receiver is tuned in to the correct frequency you will realize that the club finesse cannot possibly be the winning play. East is the one who broke radio silence. His action in winning the king of spades with his ace gave the show away. If he had a vulnerable queen of clubs in his hand he would not allow you easy access to dummy to take the finesse.

If East had three small clubs he would have good reason for wanting you to finesse in the suit. There is therefore quite a good chance that when you cash the king of clubs the queen will drop on your left.

CARD-PLACING

♠ A 3 2
♡ A Q 9 8   *Game all*
♢ A K 6
♣ K 9 4 | South | West | North | East |
                 |-------|------|-------|------|
                 | — | — | 2 NT | — |
♠ K 10 4 | 3 ♡ | — | 3 ♠ | — |
♡ K 10 6 4 2 | 4 ♣ | — | 4 ♢ | — |
♢ J 8 3 | 4 ♠ | — | 6 ♡ | all pass |
♣ A 2

West leads the knave of clubs against your six heart contract
and you win in hand with the ace. You draw trumps in three
rounds, East following while West discards a spade and a diamond. There is a disappointing duplication in your hand and
dummy's and you have no sure way of making your contract. An
elimination of some kind seems the only chance, so you play a
spade to the ace and a spade back to your king, both opponents
following with small cards. You eliminate the clubs and West
drops the ten on the third round. The ace of diamonds produces
small cards from both defenders, and you now exit with the third
round of spades, on which East plays the knave and West the
queen. West returns the ten of diamonds. Should you put up the
king or let this run to your knave?

If West has been discarding honestly he would appear to have
started with a 4–1–5–3 distribution. In that case the odds are as
good as five to two on the queen of diamonds being in the West
hand.

However, if West is a good player there is good reason to suppose that the queen, whether it will drop or not, is with East. It
would be apparent to West at an early stage that you had eleven
top tricks. Holding the queen of diamonds, he would have seen
the danger of being thrown in to lead away from it and would
have pitched his queen of spades under your king.

The proper play, therefore, is the king of diamonds.

66

CARD-PLACING

♠ K 9 7
♡ A 9 3
◇ 6 4
♣ 10 8 7 5 4

Love all

♠ A Q 8 5 3
♡ 6
◇ K Q 10 9 8 2
♣ 3

South	West	North	East
1 ◇	Double	1 NT	2 ♡
2 ♠	4 ♡	4 ♠	all pass

Against your four spade contract West leads the ace of clubs and continues with the king, East echoing with the nine and two. You ruff and play the king of diamonds. West wins with the ace and unkindly continues with the queen of clubs on which East throws the two of hearts. You ruff once again and play the queen of diamonds, both opponents following. On the third round of diamonds West plays the knave, you put in the nine of spades from dummy, and East discards the five of hearts. How do you continue?

West appears to have J 10 bare in spades and East three little ones, in which case you can simply draw trumps and make an overtrick. But there is something about the earlier play that does not quite add up. If East's distribution really was 3–6–2–2 why did he not discard a diamond on the third club? Then he could have ruffed your queen of diamonds and returned his fifth-best heart in an attempt to mislead you as to the trump distribution. East's lack of interest in a diamond ruff can only mean that he is trying to preserve a four card trump holding, in which case your one chance is that West's singleton is an honour card.

You should mutter a brief prayer and play the king of trumps from dummy, overtaking with your ace. If West drops an honour you will leave trumps and play on diamonds until East ruffs. His heart return to dummy's ace will allow you to finesse against the remaining trump honour and claim the rest of the tricks.

♠ 9 6 3
♡ K 4
◇ A K 10   *Game all*
♣ Q 10 7 6 4

South	West	North	East
—	—	1 NT	—
2 ♣	—	2 ◇	—
3 ♠	—	4 ♠	all pass

♠ A K 7 5 2
♡ Q 9 6 2
◇ J 7 3
♣ 9

Against your highly ambitious four spade contract West leads the ace of clubs and continues with the king, his partner following with the two and the three. Since this particular West normally leads the king from the top honours you take it that he is showing a doubleton by reversing the order. You ruff and lay down the ace of trumps, on which West plays the ten and East the four. How should you continue?

No doubt you are thinking harsh thoughts about your partner's raise to game, for your prospects are not good. To give you a chance the trumps will need to break 3–2 and the diamond finesse will have to be right. It looks as though West has the doubleton trump—either Q 10 or J 10. West has produced the ace and king of clubs, and you are relying on him for the queen of diamonds. If he had the ace of hearts as well he would surely have opened the bidding, so East must have that card.

It would be dangerous to lead hearts before clearing the trumps, since a club lead from East could promote an extra trump trick for the defence. Nor will it be any better to draw a second round of trumps and continue with a heart to dummy's king. East would take his ace and cash his winning trump, which would leave you a trick short.

The correct play, after winning the second round of trumps, is to lead the knave of diamonds to dummy's ace and return the four of hearts from the table. If East beats air with his ace you can afford to let him take out dummy's trump, for your remaining heart loser will be discarded on the queen of clubs.

If East plays low and permits your queen of hearts to take the trick you will still be all right. With a heart trick in the bag, the contract can be made on reverse dummy lines. You lead a diamond for a finesse of the ten, take a heart discard on the queen of clubs and ruff a club. A diamond to the king and another club ruff sees you home and dry. If East ruffs in at any time dummy's trump will be good for the tenth trick.

CHAPTER 4

Camouflage

In discussing card play in general it is fitting to refer to the skilled player as a craftsman rather than an artist. The only department of the game that can properly be described as an art is this one of camouflage and deception. Here the artist comes into his own for style is more important than technique. A player can give free rein to his imagination and express his whole personality, not only in the illusions that he fosters to ensnare his opponents but also in the manner in which he fosters them.

Do the other players in your circle regard you as a difficult opponent to play against? If not, it is time you learned how to be difficult, since a reputation for trickiness is one of the most valuable assets a player can acquire. As in poker, the main benefits accrue not when you are bluffing but when the opponents think you are bluffing and subsequently learn, to their sorrow, that you were not.

The first, and for some the hardest, lesson to be learned is of the need to control the emotions and preserve equanimity at all times. An inscrutable face is just as valuable in bridge as in poker. When disaster overtakes you in the course of play be sure that no gesture or gasp of dismay informs the defenders that you are in trouble. If they do not know how serious your position is they may find a a way of rescuing you. This applies particularly when dummy first goes down on the table. Whether dummy is a gratifying sight or a sore disappointment you should try to greet its appearance with the same unruffled composure. Any barbed remark to your partner about the lunacy of bidding on tram tickets can do nothing but help your opponents.

The player who has cultivated a deceptive style maintains an even tempo in his play whether he is dealing with a routine situation or attempting a bare-faced swindle. A fast player has a natural advantage here, for defenders are apt to get flustered if they are not given much time to think out their plays. But most declarers do not possess this happy knack of thinking and playing at great speed. Instead they must aim at consistency, taking care not to vary their pace when attempting a deception.

Since the declarer is under no obligation to convey information to his partner he does not need to follow any conventional pattern in leading or following suit. This is a great advantage, for it means he is free to select from his hand the card most calculated to cause confusion in the enemy ranks. This is not to say that declarer should play a false card automatically. Some players do just that, not realizing that wanton false-carding is worse than useless. A false card should not be played without a definite purpose in mind.

In the routine situations where the declarer wishes to confuse the enemy signals, he can save thought by remembering that he should behave exactly as though he were a defender—starting an echo if he wishes the suit to be continued, and playing his lowest card if he hopes for a switch.

Say you are playing a suit contract and West leads the ace of a side suit that he has mentioned in the bidding.

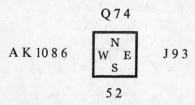

Q 7 4

A K 10 8 6   N W E S   J 9 3

5 2

By playing the five you may persuade West to continue the suit in the belief that his partner is echoing from 3 2.

If the suit is distributed as follows, on the other hand, a false card can do nothing but harm.

CAMOUFLAGE

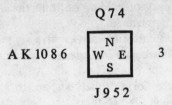

Q 7 4

A K 10 8 6   3

J 9 5 2

You want West to switch and give you a chance to pull trumps, so your proper card is the two. If you play anything else West will think that his partner is echoing.

Opportunities to jam the enemy transmissions often occur when there is a long suit in dummy and the defenders are trying to signal their length.

K Q J 8 4

7 5 3   A 10 9

6 2

At no trumps dummy has no entry and your only chance of making two tricks in this suit lies in persuading the defender who has the ace to hold off twice. By leading the six from your hand you can create some doubt in East's mind. He may read his partner for 3 2 and allow you to make your two tricks.

Conversely, in the following situation, you wish East to take his ace on the second round of the suit.

K Q J 8 4

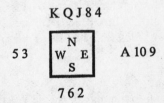

5 3   A 10 9

7 6 2

Now the only way to give East a guess is to lead the two. He will have to decide whether his partner's five is, in fact, the start of an echo, or the lowest from 7 6 5.

Note that in these positions also the declarer can keep himself right by acting as if he were a defender, echoing with a doubleton and playing his lowest card from three.

The following situation is a little more complex.

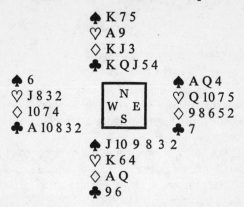

♠ K 7 5
♡ A 9
♦ K J 3
♣ K Q J 5 4

♠ 6
♡ J 8 3 2
♦ 10 7 4
♣ A 10 8 3 2

♠ A Q 4
♡ Q 10 7 5
♦ 9 8 6 5 2
♣ 7

♠ J 10 9 8 3 2
♡ K 6 4
♦ A Q
♣ 9 6

West leads the ace of clubs against your contract of four spades. Assuming East's seven to be a singleton, which card should you play from hand, the six or the nine?

The answer must depend on what you know of East's style. Many players always echo to show a doubleton even when dummy has length in the suit as here. Others do not. If East is an echoer you also must echo, playing your nine to suggest to West that his partner may have the six as well. If East does not favour the echo in this situation you should play the six.

If you don't know how East plays it you will just have to pick a card at random and pick it fast.

Enough of false-carding for the moment. Let us move on and look at some other ways of enlisting the help of the defence in making your contract.

♠ Q 10 7 4 2
♡ 6 3
◇ A 5
♣ K J 10 4

Love all

♠ K 8 6 5 3
♡ A Q 10 5
◇ J
♣ 7 5 2

South	North
1 ♠	4 ♠

West leads the six of diamonds against your four spade contract and East drops the eight under dummy's ace. How should you continue?

Assuming there is only one trump loser the contract appears to be safe unless both the queen of clubs and the king of hearts are badly placed. Can you see a way of giving yourself an extra chance if the finesses are wrong?

There is a chance that West will have the bare ace of spades, in which case, if you take away his easy exit in diamonds before putting him in, he may have an awkward guess to make. At trick two you should ruff dummy's second diamond and then lead the king of spades.

The hand cropped up in a Gold Cup match in 1964 and Kenneth Konstam earned a game swing for his team by giving an opponent the chance to go wrong. The West player, holding ♠ A, ♡ K J 8 4, ◇ Q 10 7 6 4 3, ♣ 9 6, had an unenviable decision to make when in with the ace of spades. From his point of view either a heart or a club return could be right, depending on his partner's holding in the suits. Eventually he led a heart and the hand was over.

Deceptive technique often involves no more than playing on the ignorance and the fears of your opponents. If you force them to guess they will guess wrong half of the time.

CAMOUFLAGE

♠ Q 8
♡ J 9
◇ K 7 6 5 3   *Game all*
♣ A J 9 4

	South	North
♠ K 10 9 6 5 2 | 1 ♠ | 2 ◇ |
♡ A 2 | 2 ♠ | 3 ♠ |
◇ A 8 | 4 ♠ | — |
♣ Q 3 2 | | |

West leads the six of hearts against your four spade contract and East plays the king on dummy's nine. How do you plan the play?

That's an annoying lead. On any other attack you would have chances of disposing of your heart loser. But now you must lose a heart and there is a possibility that you might lose two spades and a club as well. You could find a favourable club position, of course, or you might be able to set up enough diamond winners to take care of your losing clubs. Meanwhile how do you tackle the trumps? Should you play for the drop of the knave or take a second round finesse?

If you are accustomed to looking for ways of misleading your opponents you will not tackle trumps immediately but try to persuade the defenders to do it for you. They might be eager to do this if they thought you wanted to ruff a heart in dummy. You could win the first trick and return a heart immediately to West's queen, but West might be chary of leading a trump away from the knave and could well prefer to switch to diamonds or clubs. There is a much better chance of inducing a trump lead from East, and you should therefore play your two of hearts on the first trick.

It is quite likely that West has led from a five card or longer suit. In that case East may read you for three hearts and decide that a trump switch will be deadly.

So it will—to the defence.

CAMOUFLAGE

♠ Q 10
♡ A 7 5 4
◇ K J 7   *Love all*
♣ K 9 8 3

                  South   *North*
                  1 NT   2 ♣
♠ A J 9   2 ◇   3 NT
♡ K 6 2
◇ 10 9 6 3 2
♣ A J

West leads the five of spades against your contract of three no trumps and East plays the three under dummy's ten. How do you plan the play?

You can count six top tricks, two spades, two hearts and two clubs, and three tricks can be set up in diamonds to bring the total to nine. The only danger is that West might be able to establish his spades before you can set up the diamonds.

The unimaginative play is to win the first trick in hand with the knave and take the diamond finesse. This will meet disaster when East has the queen of diamonds and West the ace.

In this hand if the key finesse is right there is no need to take it. You can well afford to lose two diamond tricks as long as the first one is lost to West. The proper play is to allow dummy's ten to hold the first trick and lead the seven of diamonds from the table. If East holds Q x or Q x x he is likely to play low at just under the speed of light, hoping to make his queen on the next round.

If your ten of diamonds is allowed to hold the trick you should have a good chance of an overtrick. If West plays low on the next diamond you will put on dummy's king.

In theory West could defeat you on this line of play by holding up his diamond queen from Q x x. Well, if his defence is as hot as that he deserves to defeat you.

CAMOUFLAGE

♠ 8 7 2
♡ Q 4 2
♢ K 10 7 3
♣ Q 9 4

North-South game

♠ A K
♡ J 10 9 7 6 5 3
♢ A 9
♣ J 2

South	North
1 ♡	1 NT
4 ♡	—

Against your four heart contract West leads the three of spades and East plays the queen. How do you plan your play?

No doubt you are wishing you had been more conservative in the bidding, for this gamble does not look like turning out well. There is a faint legitimate chance that either opponent may have the doubleton queen and knave of diamonds, which would allow you to get a club loser away, but the main hope appears to lie in persuading the defenders to crash their trump honours.

If you play East for K x in trumps and lead the queen through him he might cover in the hope that his partner holds J x. But it is perhaps more likely that East will credit you with seven trumps on the bidding and refuse to play his king.

Prospects appear to be more hopeful if you play West for the doubleton honour. When you lead a small trump from hand he may go up from K x, or even from A x if you offer him a suitable red herring.

After winning the first trick with the ace of spades, leaving open for West the possibility of his partner having the king, you might try the effect of playing off the ace of diamonds before leading a small trump from hand.

If West believes that your ace of diamonds is single he may hasten to take his ace of trumps before you can get a loser away on dummy's king of diamonds.

CAMOUFLAGE

```
♠ K 4
♡ Q 10 6 3
◇ A K J 6 5           Game all
♣ 8 5
                      South    North
♠ A 10 7 6 2          1 ♠      2 ◇
♡ K J 2               2 NT     3 NT
◇ Q 8 2               ─
♣ A J
```

West leads the four of clubs against your three no trump contract. East produces the king and you win with the ace. How should you continue?

The contract is not a happy one in spite of your combined total of 28 points. Five diamonds would have been easier, or four hearts, or even four spades. In three no trumps you have only eight top tricks, so you will have to try to steal a heart trick at an early stage.

Assuming your opponents to be good players, what is the best way of attempting this? If East has the ace he is not likely to play low on a small heart lead from dummy. He will play the ace at once and return his partner's suit.

On this reasoning, many declarers will lead a small heart from hand at trick two, hoping to slip past the ace in the West hand. But this play has no better chance. West will wonder why you are not playing on diamonds. If he concludes that your diamonds are solid he will realize that his only chance is to play the ace of hearts at once and lay down the club queen.

Although you must hope that West has the ace of hearts, you should play as though you are trying to slip past *East's* ace, for that would be normal play if you had knave and another club left. At the second trick you should lead the eight of diamonds (concealing the two) to dummy's king and return a heart to your king. On winning with the ace West may well lead a red suit in an attempt to put his partner in.

CAMOUFLAGE

♠ A 7 4 3
♡ J 8 3
◇ K Q
♣ 8 5 4 2

Game all

	South	West	North	East
♠ Q 10 9 8 6 5 2	3 ♠	3 NT	4 ♠	—
♡ 4	—	Double	all pass	
◇ J 9 5				
♣ A Q				

West starts off with the two top hearts against your doubled contract of four spades. After ruffing the second round how should you continue?

West's three no trump bid was a request for a takeout but, in view of his final double, he is quite likely to have the king and knave of spades. That means that you have four probable losers, since the club finesse must be wrong.

There are elimination possibilities, though, and it must be right to lead a diamond at trick three. When you do so West takes his ace and returns the queen of hearts, forcing you to ruff again. Now what?

That third round of hearts has unfortunately removed dummy's exit card and made it impossible for you to eliminate the diamonds before throwing West in with the second round of spades. There is just one little ruse left to try. You should lead your knave of diamonds to dummy's king in the hope of inducing West to miscount your hand. You next cash the ace of trumps and when East shows out continue with a second trump to put West in. If he believes that you started with only two diamonds and therefore three clubs he may make the greedy return of a club, hoping to find his partner with the queen and collect a 500 penalty.

The defenders should not go wrong in such situations, of course, but they often do. Anyway, there's no law against trying.

CAMOUFLAGE

♠ J742
♡ K843
♢ Q9
♣ A52

♠ A9653
♡ 6
♢ KJ1063
♣ K9

Love all

West	North	East	South
—	—	1 NT*	2 ♠
—	3 ♠	—	4 ♠
all pass			

12–14 points

West leads the queen of hearts against your four spade contract. On your play of a low card from dummy East drops the seven, and West continues with the knave of hearts which you ruff. How do you plan the play?

There will be no trouble if the trumps break 2–2, but what if they are 3–1? Then you will have a technical choice of two plays, either of which might limit your trump losers to one trick. You could cater for a singleton king or queen in East's hand by cashing the ace of spades first, or you could play West for the singleton ten.

In view of the bidding East can hardly have a singleton spade, whether an honour or not, but West could quite well have the bare ten. The correct play, therefore, is to cross to dummy with the ace of clubs and lead the knave of spades, running it if East plays low.

Curiously enough the correct technical play is also the best deceptive play in this case. If East's trump holding is K 10 8 or Q 10 8 he will have a difficult decision to make when the knave is led from dummy. From his point of view it would be correct to cover the knave if you have three side-suit losers and West the bare nine of trumps.

If East does cover from such a holding he will finish up with only one trump trick and a pair of red ears.

CAMOUFLAGE

♠ 8 7 3 2
♡ A 9 4 2
◇ 8 4   *Game all*
♣ A J 9

♠ A K
♡ K 10 6 5 3
◇ A K Q J
♣ 8 6

South	North
1 ♡	3 ♡
6 ♡	—

West leads the king of clubs against your contract of six hearts and you win with dummy's ace. How should you continue?

The opening lead has hit you in your weak spot and put paid to any ideas of safety-playing the trumps, but you may not have to lose a trump trick. If you play the trump ace from dummy and West drops an honour card, or if you play a small trump to your king and East plays an honour, you will have to choose between playing for the drop and finessing on the second round. The choice is not even close, of course. Playing for the drop gives by far the best chance. If the trumps break 2–2 you will make all thirteen tricks, while if it transpires that you have a trump loser you will still make your contract if the defender with three trumps also has three or more diamonds, for you will be able to get dummy's club losers away.

The correct play is to lead a small trump to your king at trick two and return a trump to dummy's ace. There is a subtle reason for wishing the lead to be in dummy after two rounds of trumps. Should West prove to have a trump winner you can give yourself an additional chance if he has only two diamonds. By leading a diamond to your queen, cashing the diamond ace and continuing with the knave you may give West the impression that you have finessed against his partner's king. If he declines to waste his master trump on the 'losing' knave of diamonds, you will succeed in making an impossible contract.

CAMOUFLAGE

♠ 8 5
♡ 10 9 7 2
◇ A 3
♣ K 8 7 4 3

Game all

	West	North	East	South
			1 ◇	Double
♠ A Q 6 2	1 NT	2 ♣	—	2 ♡
♡ A Q J 6 5 3	—	4 ♡	all pass	
◇ 7 6				
♣ J				

West leads the four of hearts against your four heart contract. You play the ten from dummy and East, looking cross, discards the king of diamonds. How do you plan the play?

There is a certain loser in trumps and a possible loser in each of the other suits. Perhaps it is just as well for you that West failed to lead his partner's suit for you now have a chance of discarding your diamond loser on the king of clubs.

One way of tackling the problem would be to win the first trick in your hand and lead the knave of clubs through West, going up with the king if he plays small. However, if you have worked your way through the card-placing problems in the previous chapter you will realize that if West has the ace of clubs your contract is in no danger anyway, for then East will assuredly have the king of spades.

The dangerous case is where West has the king of spades and East the ace of clubs. You should therefore allow dummy's ten to win the first trick and put East immediately to the test by leading the three of clubs from the table. If East has the ace without the queen he will have an agonizing guess to make. For all he knows your hand could well be ♠ A Q x x, ♡ A K J x x, ◇ x x x, ♣ Q, in which case it would be fatal for him to duck.

If East puts on his ace you can sit back in comfort and enjoy the post-mortem.

CAMOUFLAGE

♠ A Q 8 3
♡ J 9 6 5
◇ —
♣ K Q 7 4 3

East-West game

♠ J 5
♡ K 8
◇ 10 7 2
♣ A 10 9 8 6 2

West	North	East	South
1 ◇	Double	2 ◇	4 ♣
—	5 ♣	all pass	

West leads the ace of diamonds against your five club contract. How do you plan the play?

The contract is in no danger unless the spade finesse is wrong and the ace and queen of hearts are behind the king. You have no particular reason to suppose this to be the case, but if East has the king of spades West will certainly have the ace of hearts and could well have the queen.

In fact this is another case where if the key finesse is right there is no need to take it. After ruffing the ace of diamonds in dummy you should play off the ace of spades and continue with the three of spades from the table. If East has the king it is unlikely that he will play it. From your line of play he will be convinced that you are going to ruff this trick. If the spade king should turn up in the West hand after all, your contract will still be safe. No return West may make can harm you, and you will later be able to discard a heart from your hand on dummy's queen of spades.

In this hand, as in many where deceptive measures offer the best chance, it is important to make the key play at an early stage. To draw a round of trumps before playing spades could be fatal, for it would give East a chance to assess your strength and distribution. Once he realized that the defence had no trump trick and not more than two hearts to make he would have no hesitation in playing his king of spades on the second round of the suit.

CAMOUFLAGE

♠ K 10 5
♡ J 4
◇ Q 9 7 6 2
♣ A K 8

Game all

West	North	East	South
1 ♡	Double	1 ♠	3 NT
all pass			

♠ Q 3
♡ K Q 7
◇ K 4
♣ Q 10 9 6 3 2

West leads the nine of spades against your three no trump contract. How should you plan the play?

You note with regret that you are playing this contract from the wrong side of the table. Perhaps you should have bid the opponents' suits in an effort to persuade your partner to call notrumps. That would certainly have worked better on this hand, for nine tricks would be practically a certainty if North were the declarer.

This awkward spade lead from West puts you in serious danger of defeat. East will no doubt allow your queen of spades to win the first trick, and when West gets in with the ace of hearts a further spade lead will give his partner four or five tricks in the suit.

The one factor working in your favour on this hand is East's ignorance of the weakness of your position. You should try to make capital out of this by playing exactly as though you had another small spade in your hand. In other words, you should play the king of spades from dummy on the first trick.

East will be most unlikely to duck for fear of allowing you to make two spade tricks. For the same reason, on winning with the ace, he will be almost certain to switch to hearts, hoping to set up some tricks for his partner. And a heart switch will suit you just fine.

A stopper, as Shakespeare might have said, is neither weak nor strong but thinking makes it so.

CAMOUFLAGE

♠ A Q 5
♡ 6
◇ Q 10 9 5 2
♣ K 9 8 3

Love all

	South	North
	1 NT	2 NT
	3 NT	—

♠ J 8 6
♡ K J 4 2
◇ A J 7 3
♣ A 4

West leads the seven of hearts against your contract of three no trumps and East plays the ten. How should you plan the play?

The contract is reasonable enough and should be made unless your luck is really bad. Five diamond tricks, along with four certain tricks in the other suits, will see you home. Even if the diamond finesse is wrong you will still be all right if the king of spades is with West. So it looks as though your contract depends on one of two finesses being right, which gives you approximately a 75 per cent chance of success. Is there anything you can do to cater for the remaining 25 per cent zone where both finesses are wrong?

You can, in fact, improve your chances considerably by winning the first trick with the king of hearts rather than the knave. Next you will lead a club to dummy's king and try the diamond finesse. If it fails there is a good chance that West will go wrong now. Unless he has a very suspicious mind he will believe that the heart suit is his to run. He will either lead a low heart to the knave he imagines his partner to hold, or play his hearts from the top down, expecting his partner to unblock.

In either case the knave of hearts will provide your ninth trick.

CAMOUFLAGE

♠ 8 7 4
♡ K Q
◇ 6 4
♣ K 9 8 6 3 2

Game all

	South	North
	2 ♣	3 ♣
♠ K 10	4 ♣	5 ♣
♡ A 7 5 2	6 ♣	—
◇ A K J		
♣ A Q J 10		

West leads the knave of hearts against your six club contract. How do you plan the play?

It looks as though your slam is a 50 per cent chance and will make only if the spade ace is with East. You could, of course, take the diamond finesse instead of playing spades, but that would still give you no more than a fifty-fifty chance. The only other possibility is to play West for both the ace of spades and the queen of diamonds and strip-squeeze him, but that will succeed only 24 per cent of the time.

Many players will not realize that in playing on spades they can give themselves an extra chance even if the ace is behind the king. First it is necessary to feed West some false information about the distribution of your hand.

After winning the first trick with the queen of hearts you should lead a trump to your ace and draw the rest of the enemy trumps. Then cash the ace of hearts, crashing dummy's king, and play off the ace, king and knave of diamonds, ruffing the third round in dummy. The stage is now set for a spade lead to your king.

If West holds something like A J x x in spades he could not be censured for ducking this trick. It would certainly be wrong for him to take his ace if your original hand really was ♠ K Q 10 x, ♡ A x, ◇ A K J, ♣ A Q J 10, for he would then be end-played, forced either to return a spade up to your tenace holding or concede a ruff and discard.

CAMOUFLAGE

♠ K 7 4
♡ K J 7 3
◇ K Q 8 4
♣ 10 4

Game all—Pairs

West	North	East	South
		1 ♠	2 ♡
2 ♠	4 ♡	4 ♠	5 ♡
Double	all pass		

♠ 10
♡ A Q 10 9 6 5 2
◇ 6
♣ A J 9 7

In an expert game, West leads the two of spades against your doubled contract of five hearts. How do you plan the play?

Prospects are not at all bright and you are no doubt wishing you had passed and allowed your partner to double four spades. You have a loser in each of the three side suits, and even if West has the ace of diamonds it is unlikely that he will allow you to slip a diamond through. But for the moment there is nothing else to try.

Since you hope for a spade continuation rather than a diamond or club switch, you play dummy's king of spades on the first trick. East wins with the ace and duly returns a spade which you ruff. You try the six of diamonds but, as you feared, West goes up with the ace and leads another spade, forcing you to ruff again. Now what?

You have ten sure tricks and technically no chance at all of making an eleventh. There can be no squeeze because dummy has no side entry. At this stage most players would draw trumps, discard two clubs on dummy's king and queen of diamonds, and then run the rest of the trumps, conceding a club trick at the end for one down and a poor match-point score.

An imaginative declarer who is accustomed to looking at problems from the opponents' point of view may see the ghost of a chance of making his contract, however. Once again your one asset is the defenders' ignorance of your distribution. They do not know your diamond was a singleton. Should the diamonds break 4-4 it is possible that each defender will believe that he alone is capable of preventing you from making three diamond tricks.

After ruffing the third round of spades you should ignore

dummy's diamonds and play out all your trumps. When the pressure ceases you may be lucky enough to find both the king and the queen of clubs dropping under your ace.

This type of bluff squeeze occurs more often in print than at the table, and it is pleasant to be able to record that the hand is taken from play. The occasion was the *Sunday Times* Invitation Pairs Tournament of 1966, and the successful declarer C. Slavenburg of the Netherlands.

The full hand was as follows.

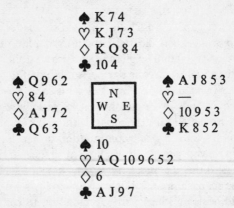

```
                    ♠ K 7 4
                    ♡ K J 7 3
                    ◇ K Q 8 4
                    ♣ 10 4
  ♠ Q 9 6 2                        ♠ A J 8 5 3
  ♡ 8 4          N                 ♡ —
  ◇ A J 7 2    W   E               ◇ 10 9 5 3
  ♣ Q 6 3         S                ♣ K 8 5 2
                    ♠ 10
                    ♡ A Q 10 9 6 5 2
                    ◇ 6
                    ♣ A J 9 7
```

It is hard to blame the defenders for being taken in, although East might have come up with the right answer if he had asked himself, before playing to the last trump, why his partner had not discarded a diamond.

CHAPTER 5

Good and Bad Breaks

Players who are consistently successful are often accused of being lucky. Many people appear to have the impression that the cards break better for good players than for lesser mortals. It is not true of course. The expert finds himself faced with a 5–0 trump break just as often as anyone else, and if his finesses seem to fail less frequently it is only because he takes fewer finesses than the average player. What gives the good player his edge is that he has acquired the habit of looking ahead and anticipating the dangers that may arise. This often enables him to minimize the effect of bad breaks.

Should you feel that you have been getting more than your share of unlucky breaks recently, if your seemingly cast-iron contracts show an alarming tendency to founder on the rocks of distribution, then the chances are that you need to brush up your safety technique.

The safety principle has a wide application over the whole

range of dummy play. The term 'safety play' embraces the simple precautionary measures that cost nothing, and also the true insurance plays wherein a trick is sacrificed, perhaps unnecessarily, in order to guard against a hypothetical bad break. In certain cases safety play will make your contract unbeatable; in others it can do more than improve your chances.

When a hand looks simple that is the time to be especially watchful. It is fatally easy to embark on a happy-go-lucky line of play after a cursory analysis. Good breaks should never be taken for granted if there is any way of protecting yourself against bad ones. On those hands where it looks as though it will take a thunderbolt to defeat your contract you must ask yourself where the thunderbolt is likely to strike and what you can do about it. If you expect the worst you will not be taken unawares.

Before indulging in safety play, however, remember that it is a luxury. When you have plenty of winners and would normally expect to make overtricks you can no doubt well afford to pay the premium on a safety play policy. But paupers cannot afford insurance. Perhaps your partner has overbid and your contract is dangerously high. In that case there is no question of catering for bad breaks. Instead you must hope for good ones. When the situation is really desperate you will have to pray for miracles. If there is one distribution of the opponents' cards that will allow you to make your contract you must play for it, no matter how improbable it may be.

To be a successful dummy-player, then, you will have to exercise both boldness and caution as the occasion demands. When prospects look good your attitude must be pessimistic, but when your cause appears hopeless you must be a super-optimist. It is because safety play and desperation play are opposite sides of the same medal that both types of play are lumped together in this chapter.

The ways of handling different card combinations for maximum safety are known well enough. The problems that follow are concerned not so much with standard safety plays in a single suit as with the application of the safety principle to the hand as a whole.

GOOD AND BAD BREAKS

Here is a straightforward example.

♠ 9 8 6
♡ 6 5 3
◇ Q J 8 7   *East-West game*
♣ A 3 2

	West	North	East	South
	1 ♣	—	2 ♣	4 ♡
	all pass			

♠ A K 4
♡ A K J 10 9 7 4
◇ 6 2
♣ 5

Against your four heart contract West leads the ace of diamonds and then hastily switches to the king of clubs in order to knock out dummy's ace. How do you plan the play?

The contract is a sound one. On a normal 2–1 trump break eleven tricks are there for the taking. After drawing trumps you can knock out the king of diamonds and dummy's third trump will provide entry to the table for you to discard your spade loser on dummy's winning diamond.

When it looks as easy as this you must ask yourself what could possibly go wrong. Well, if the trumps break 3–0 you could lose a trump and two diamonds, and you would have to lose a spade as well for there will now be no entry to dummy. What can be done about it? Nothing if the trumps are with West, but if East has all three trumps a simple finesse will protect you. Since dummy has no other entry you will have to take that finesse straight away.

If East follows to the lead of the three of trumps from dummy you can make certain of your contract by playing the knave from your hand. Should West win this trick it means that dummy's third trump will serve as an entry and you will lose no spade trick, while if West shows out you have no trump loser.

This play will cost you the overtrick when West has the bare queen of trumps or queen and another. That is the modest premium you pay for ensuring ten tricks when West is void.

♠ K 10 7 6 3
♡ A Q 9 4
♦ 10   *Love all*
♣ J 7 4

	South	North
♠ A	1 ◊	1 ♠
♡ 10 6	3 ◊	3 ♡
♦ K Q J 7 6 5 2	3 NT	—
♣ A 10 3		

West leads the five of clubs against your three no trump contract. East plays the queen and you win with the ace. How do you plan the play?

Perhaps you should have bid five diamonds, but that contract would have had its own problems, especially on a heart lead. In three no trumps the only real chance—apart from a couple of way-out possibilities—is to bring in the long diamonds. You should therefore concentrate on playing the diamond suit to the best advantage.

If you lead a small card to dummy's ten the opponents will almost certainly hold up the ace and you will be unable to establish the suit for lack of entries to your hand. It must be much better to lead the king of diamonds from hand at the second trick. This will ensure success if the diamonds break no worse than 3–2.

It is possible to obtain an additional margin of safety, however. The correct play is to lead the six of hearts to dummy's ace and return the ten of diamonds from the table, overtaking in your hand if East plays low. This play still wins when the diamonds are 3–2 and it also succeeds when East has the singleton ace. This gives you an extra 2·8 per cent chance of success. Not a great deal, perhaps, but the ability to marshal such small extra percentages in your favour can make quite a difference to your score-sheet.

GOOD AND BAD BREAKS

♠ A 6 4 3
♡ A J 8 7 3
♢ 9 4   *North-South game*
♣ J 9

South	North
1 ♣	1 ♡
1 ♠	3 ♠
4 ♣	—

♠ K Q J 9
♡ 5
♢ Q 7
♣ A K 10 8 6 2

West leads the five of diamonds against your four spade contract, East winning with the ace and returning the two to his partner's king. West switches to the four of hearts and you win with dummy's ace. You play a trump to your king and continue with the queen, East discarding a diamond on the second round. What should you do now?

Without the annoying 4–1 trump break the contract would have been simple to fulfil. You have still good chances of course. If the clubs break 3–2 you will have no worries, for you can ruff the third round with the ace of trumps, return dummy's last trump to your knave, and play clubs until West takes his master trump.

There is danger in that line if the clubs break badly, however. If you play out the top two clubs and West ruffs the second round you will probably be held to eight tricks.

This is another case where a possible overtrick has to be sacrificed in order to make sure of the contract. The safe way to continue is to cash the club ace, throwing the knave from dummy, and follow with the club ten from your hand. The unblocking play is necessary in case East, with four clubs to the queen, holds off on the second round. No matter which opponent wins the second round of clubs your contract is safe. On a heart or diamond return you will ruff in hand and ram the club suit through West. When he decides to ruff in you can over-ruff with dummy's ace and draw West's last trump as you return to hand to run the rest of the clubs.

GOOD AND BAD BREAKS

```
♠ K 9 6 2
♡ 9 4
◇ A Q 8 5                    Game all
♣ J 6 5
                     South    West    North    East
♠ Q J 10 8 4          1 ♠    Double   2 NT     —
♡ A 10               4 ♠    all pass
◇ K 7 2
♣ K 9 3
```

West leads the king of hearts against your four spade contract. How do you plan the play?

When you see the unfortunate duplication in dummy you wish you had taken a less optimistic view in the bidding and settled for three spades. Nine tricks appear to be there all right, but on this lead it is hard to see where the tenth might come from. It is no good hoping for the ace of clubs to be favourably placed, for West must surely have that card to justify his vulnerable double.

This is no occasion for safety play, of course. When your contract looks almost impossible the only thing to do is to dream up some helpful distribution of the opponents' cards and play on the assumption that that distribution actually exists. Here the only hope is that you can throw West in to lead away from his ace of clubs, and for that to be possible the diamonds will have to break evenly and West must have the singleton ace of spades. Not a very good chance, perhaps, but it is the only one you have.

You should therefore play three rounds of diamonds before leading a spade. If West has the hand you hope for, something like ♠ A, ♡ K Q J x x, ◇ x x x, ♣ A 10 x x, he will be able to cash a heart but will then either have to open up the club suit or give you a ruff and discard. Even if West does not have the knave of hearts he may be afraid to underlead his queen to put his partner in.

GOOD AND BAD BREAKS

♠ Q 10 4 3
♡ Q
♢ Q J 9 6 3
♣ Q 10 6

Love all

South	North
1 ♣	1 ♢
3 NT	—

♠ K 8 5
♡ A J 9
♢ K 7 2
♣ A K J 4

West leads the six of hearts against your three no trump contract, East covers dummy's queen with the king and your ace wins. How should you continue?

In spite of your impressive combined point-count you have only six top winners and need to develop three more. If the diamonds behave kindly you will have no worries, of course, but it would be unwise to bank on a favourable diamond break. East could have A 10 x x, in which case you will be unable to make more than two diamond tricks, for as soon as you let East in a heart will come through your J 9. Can you see a way of guarding against this dangerous diamond distribution?

It is all a matter of timing your sequence of plays so that East cannot obtain the lead too early. At trick two you should lead your small club to dummy's ten and return the three of diamonds towards your king. If East beats air with his ace you have your nine tricks, while if West wins he can do you no harm. Should the king of diamonds hold the trick the safe continuation is to go back to dummy with the club queen and lead a small spade to your king. Once again East cannot play the ace without giving you nine tricks, while if West produces the ace and leads another spade you will play dummy's queen and set up the other trick you need in diamonds. Similarly, if the king of spades wins, you will switch back to diamonds for your ninth trick.

Careful play thus makes the contract unbeatable.

♠ 10 5 3 2
♡ A   *Game all*
◇ J 10 6
♣ A Q J 10 7

	South	North
	1 ♠	3 ♣
♠ A Q J 4	4 ♣	4 ♠
♡ 9 8 3	5 ◇	5 ♡
◇ A Q 4	6 ♠	—
♣ K 8 2		

West leads the queen of hearts against your six spade contract. How do you plan the play?

This is a perfectly good slam to be in. If you can manage to ruff two hearts in dummy you will be able to get your diamond losers away on the clubs and will not need to take the diamond finesse. Only a bad trump break will complicate matters. You will be unable to cope with a 5–0 break, but what if the trumps are 4–1?

If West has four trumps to the king he will no doubt refuse to win the first round. When you lead a second round he will take his king and return a trump, which will stop you ruffing two hearts and force you to fall back on the diamond finesse.

But if East has the four trumps you will always be able to make your contract provided that you force him to take his trump trick on the first round.

The proper play is to lead the ten of spades from dummy at trick two, allowing East to hold the trick if he covers with the king. This safety play gives up the chance of an overtrick, but you will now be able to negotiate the heart ruffs you need without difficulty, even on a 4–1 trump break. If East returns a diamond you will put on the ace, ruff a heart, return with a trump and ruff your last heart. Then back to your king of clubs to draw the outstanding trumps and claim the contract.

♠ A Q 2
♡ K
♢ Q 5 4 3 2   *North-South game*
♣ A Q 5 3

West	North	East	South
—	1 ◊	—	3 NT
—	6 NT	all pass	

♠ 10 7 4 3
♡ A Q 4
♢ A K 6
♣ K 9 6

West leads the three of hearts against your six no trump contract and East follows with the two. You play a diamond from dummy to your ace and West discards the five of spades. How should you continue?

The bad diamond break has made the hand more difficult, but you can be thankful that you avoided a six diamond contract. In six no trumps you have only ten top tricks, and it looks as though you will need the spade finesse plus either a club break or a black suit squeeze.

If West's opening lead was honest he must have started with nine black cards, either six spades and three clubs or five spades and four clubs, to judge from his discard. Whichever holding he has, the correct play at trick three must be a spade to dummy's ace to guard against a possible singleton king with East. If East follows with a small card you can return to the king of diamonds and lead another spade towards dummy. Should West again play low and East show out, you will be able to rectify the count for the squeeze by playing a small diamond from dummy. Whatever East returns after winning this trick, you will enter dummy in clubs and cash the queen of diamonds, discarding a spade from hand, then return to the king of clubs to cash the hearts and inflict the squeeze on West.

This hand was played in the U.S. 1964 Olympiad Trials, and the thoughtful safety play of the ace of spades at trick three was made by Lew Mathe.

♠ K J 10 9
♡ 10
◇ K J 9 5 3   *East-West game*
♣ Q 10 4
                     South   *North*
                     1 NT   2 ♣
♠ Q 7   2 ◇   2 NT
♡ Q J 6   3 NT   —
◇ A 10 8
♣ A 8 7 5 2

West leads the five of hearts against your three no trump contract and East drops the eight under dummy's ten. How should you plan the play?

This looks horrible. No doubt your partner thought that his nines and tens made it worth while to try for game, but you would have been much happier playing in two diamonds.

Prospects in three no trumps are very bleak. Even if you guess the diamond position correctly you will have no more than seven top tricks. The opponents have at least four heart winners to run as soon as they get in. That they will allow you to slip past the ace of spades twice is altogether too much to hope for.

There is only one real chance—a slender one, but you must play for it. You should base your plan on the expectancy of making one heart trick, five diamonds and three clubs. That means that East must have the singleton king of clubs. There is no other way of doing it.

If East is short in clubs he is likely to have length in diamonds, so at trick two you should play a small diamond from dummy and finesse your eight. If that goes well you cross your fingers and lay down the ace of clubs. When East's king drops you will be able to finesse against West's knave, take a second diamond finesse, cash the diamond ace, and return to the table with the queen of clubs to make the remaining diamonds.

GOOD AND BAD BREAKS

♠ A Q 6 5
♡ 4
◇ K 8 6 3
♣ J 8 6 5

Love all

	South	North
	1 ♠	3 ♠
	4 ♠	—

♠ K J 8 7 2
♡ A J
◇ Q 5 4 2
♣ A 4

West leads the king of hearts against your four spade contract and your ace wins the trick. How should you continue?

Confronted with this hand at the table, ninety-nine players out of a hundred would see nothing better to do than ruff the knave of hearts immediately and draw as many rounds of trumps as necessary before tackling the diamonds. Most of the time the contract will be made, and the ninety-nine players will pass on to the next hand unaware that they have misplayed this one.

Anyone can make this contract if the diamonds break normally. The problem is to recognize that the hand can still be made if the diamonds are 4–1 provided that the trumps are 2–2 and you take the proper precautions in time.

The correct procedure is to test the trumps at trick two by leading a spade to dummy's queen. When both opponents follow you should continue with a club to the ace and a second round of clubs. If East wins this trick and leads another club you can afford to ruff high. Now you play a second round of trumps to dummy's ace and if both opponents follow you are home. Another club ruff in your hand is followed by a heart ruff in dummy and then a low diamond from both hands. If the diamonds do in fact break 4–1 or worse whoever wins this trick will be end-played, compelled either to concede a ruff and discard or to allow you to make two diamond tricks.

GOOD AND BAD BREAKS

♠ J 4
♡ K 9 3
♢ 10 4
♣ K Q 10 7 6 2

Game all

South	North
2 ♡	4 ♡
6 ♡	—

♠ A K 10 6 2
♡ A Q 10 8 6 4
♢ 7
♣ A

Unscientific bidding, no doubt, but at least it has not given West any help for he leads the nine of spades against your six heart contract. You gratefully put up dummy's knave, East covers with the queen and your ace wins. It looks plain sailing now, but when you cash the ace of hearts East discards the nine of diamonds and the contract becomes awkward. You play off the club ace, enter dummy by finessing the nine of hearts, and discard your diamond on the king of clubs while both opponents follow suit. How should you continue?

You still have two losing spades to dispose of. If you can ruff one of them with the king of trumps you will be able to discard the other on the queen of clubs, and all the defence will make is a trump trick. However, it would be highly dangerous to lead a spade now for West might ruff and return his last trump. You would then be a trick short unless the clubs break evenly. For the same reason it would be just as dangerous to continue with the queen of clubs. If West ruffed and returned his last trump you would be one down.

What you have to find is a play that will cater for West now being void in either black suit. The proper play is to lead a small club from the table and ruff low in your hand. If West over-ruffs no return can hurt you since the clubs are now established, while if West follows to the third round of clubs or refuses to over-ruff you can safely continue with the king of spades and make sure of your spade ruff.

♠ K 6 4
♡ 9 6 5
◇ Q 5
♣ A K Q 8 3

North-South game

South	North
1 ♠	2 ♣
2 ♠	4 ♠

♠ A Q 7 3 2
♡ Q 8
◇ A J 7
♣ 10 9 5

West leads the two of hearts against your four spade contract. East takes the ace and returns the three of hearts to his partner's king, and West continues with the knave of hearts which you ruff. How do you plan the play?

There will be eleven tricks for the taking if both spades and clubs behave reasonably, so assume that they don't. It is easy enough to cater for a 4–1 trump break as long as the first two trumps are won in hand. If either defender shows out you switch to clubs to force out the other defender's second last trump, and the king of spades will provide access to the good clubs on the table. But suppose the clubs are 4–1 as well?

To play this hand for maximum safety requires a well-timed sequence of plays. The correct method is to lead the ten of clubs to dummy's ace, return a small trump to your ace, and continue with the nine of clubs. If West ruffs ahead of dummy you will have no further problem, but if West discards it probably means that he has the rest of the trumps. In that case you will need the diamond finesse to be right and you might as well take it straight away. If West follows to the second round of clubs your contract is assured. You play the king from dummy and if East also follows you can proceed as planned, leading a second trump to your queen to guard against a 4–1 trump break. If East started with four trumps and a singleton club he will probably not ruff the second round of clubs, but it makes no difference. A trump to your queen followed by the marked finesse of the eight of clubs will leave East helpless.

GOOD AND BAD BREAKS

```
♠ Q 3
♡ A Q 5
◇ K 8 6 5                     North-South game
♣ A J 7 3
                        West    North   East    South
                                          —       —
♠ J 7 2                 1 ♠    Double   2 ◇     3 ♣
♡ K J 8                  —      3 ♠      —      3 NT
◇ A 3                   all pass
♣ 10 9 8 5 4
```

West starts with the six of spades against your three no trump
contract. You play low from dummy and East puts in the ten.
How do you plan the play?

This looks grim. There are only seven top tricks and the extra
tricks you require can come only from the club suit. But as soon
as you let the opponents in they are sure to run enough spade
tricks to defeat you.

Ask yourself the usual question. Is there any conceivable distribution of the enemy cards that will enable you to make your contract? Could West have seven spades and no outside entry, for
instance? That is unlikely for two reasons. With seven spades
headed by the ace and king West would probably have opened
with a three bid. Also he would be unlikely to underlead his
honours with that holding.

There is one other remote possibility. East could have exactly
two spades, the king and the ten, along with one of the club
honours. In that case if you win the first trick with your knave and
play on clubs East will win the trick and lead his king of spades
for West to overtake. But if you refuse to play your knave on the
first trick the spade suit will be blocked, and you will be able to
keep West out of the lead by finessing in clubs.

As the only chance, therefore, you should play the two of
spades on the first trick.

102

GOOD AND BAD BREAKS

♠ K J 4
♡ A J 9 3
◇ 10 5 2   *Game all*
♣ Q J 9

           South   *North*

♠ A 10 2   1 ♡   2 NT
♡ K Q 10 7 6 4 4 ♡   —
◇ K 7 4 3
♣ —

West leads the five of clubs against your four heart contract. East plays the king on dummy's nine and you ruff. Both defenders follow suit when you lead a small trump to dummy's ace. How should you continue?

It looks as though East has the ace of clubs as well as the king, in which case after drawing a second round of trumps you will be able to run dummy's queen of clubs and discard a spade from your hand.

But although it is certainly unlikely that West would underlead the ace of clubs at trick one, you cannot be quite sure that he did not do so. If West were to produce the ace of clubs and return a club you might find that you still had to lose three diamond tricks and the contract.

A second best line of play should not be considered when absolute safety is available. The proper way to play the hand is to ruff a club at trick three, return to dummy with the trump knave, and ruff out the last club. At this stage you have only one trump left in your hand and you cannot afford to use it to enter dummy in order to lead a diamond towards your king. You don't need to do that anyway. The play of a low diamond from both hands is perfectly safe. If East wins and returns a diamond you will again play low, but if he now leads a third diamond you must cover with the king. Should West be able to win this trick it means that the diamonds have broken evenly, and that is the end of the defence.

♠ 6 4
♡ A 10 9 3
♢ 9 5 3
♣ A K 10 6   *North-South game*

♠ K J 7   *South* *West* *North* *East*
♡ Q J 7 5   1 ♡   1 ♠   4 ♡   all pass
♢ A K
♣ Q 8 5 2

West leads the knave of clubs against your four heart contract. How should you plan the play?

On the bidding the heart finesse could easily be right, but it wouldn't do to bank on it. You can afford to lose a trump trick and two spades, of course, but the trouble is that this knave of clubs may be a singleton. In that case, if East has the king of hearts you could suffer a club ruff and lose four tricks altogether.

Perhaps it would be as well to abandon the trump finesse on this hand, playing ace and another instead. That will settle West's hash if he has two small trumps, but if he has three he will still get his club ruff and then exit with a diamond and wait for his spade tricks.

The safest method of dealing with this hand is by means of a semi-elimination. You should play off the ace and king of diamonds, cross to the ace of hearts, and ruff dummy's third diamond before leading a second round of trumps. Now if East wins and returns a club for his partner to ruff, West will have no safe exit card left. He will either have to give you a ruff and discard or allow you to make a spade trick.

It is true that you could go down on this line of play if East has four trumps to the king, but it is not always possible to cater for every eventuality. The indications in this case are that an adverse club ruff is a greater danger than a bad trump break.

♠ Q 9 6
♡ A 9 3
♢ 7 5 4
♣ A 7 4 2   *Game all*

♠ A 10 8 5 3   *South*   *West*   *North*   *East*
♡ J   1 ♠   4 ♡   4 ♠   all pass
♢ K J 10
♣ Q J 10 3

West leads the king of hearts against your four spade contract. You put on dummy's ace, but to your annoyance East ruffs with the two of spades and returns the nine of diamonds. You try the knave but West produces the queen and cashes the ace of diamonds before exiting with the queen of hearts. How should you plan the play?

No doubt you are rehearsing some choice phrases in which to tell your partner exactly what you think of his four spade bid on that horrible flat hand. But forget it for the moment and concentrate on the contract, for your partner will not listen meekly to a lecture on bidding if you fail to take any available chance to make your game.

Prospects are certainly extremely poor. Having lost three tricks already you need to take all the rest, but there are potential losers in both trumps and clubs.

At least West's long heart suit makes it fairly easy to count the hand and work out where your only hope lies. West started with nine hearts and two diamonds that you know of, therefore he cannot have more than two cards in spades and clubs. To give you a chance he must have two very specific singletons—the knave of spades and the king of clubs. There is no other way of avoiding a loser in the black suits.

You should therefore lead the three of clubs to dummy's ace and return the queen of spades to pin West's knave.

♠ 7 4
♡ 9 5 4   *Game all*
◇ Q 8 7 6 3
♣ K 6 2

South	North
2 ♠	2 NT
3 ♣	3 ◇
3 ♠	4 ♠

♠ A Q J 10 6
♡ 8 2
◇ A K
♣ A Q J 5

After the bidding it is no great surprise when West leads the three of hearts against your four spade contract. East wins with the ace and returns the six to his partner's knave. West continues with the king of hearts, East plays the ten and you ruff. How should you proceed?

You have plenty of tricks to make and there will be no trouble if the trumps break 3–3, for you will then be able to afford a spade loser. There could be danger when the trumps are 4–2, however, for when the defender with the king of spades gets in he will lead another heart to force you, thereby establishing another trump trick for the defence.

It is not possible to achieve absolute safety on this hand. If West has four trumps to the king and defends properly you are doomed to defeat. But correct play will enable you to cope with the case where East has the four trumps to the king.

At trick four you should lead the queen of spades from hand. If either opponent wins this trick your contract is safe, for the opposing hearts appear to be distributed 4–4 and dummy's spade will protect you from a heart force.

If the queen of spades is allowed to win you should cross to the table with the king of clubs and lead dummy's spade for a finesse. When your spade knave holds the trick you will continue with the ace, and if the spades now fail to break you can abandon trumps and gather in ten tricks by playing on the side suits.

GOOD AND BAD BREAKS

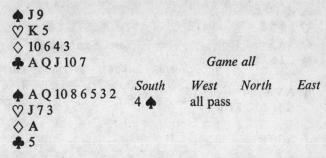

♠ J 9
♡ K 5
◇ 10 6 4 3
♣ A Q J 10 7   *Game all*

♠ A Q 10 8 6 5 3 2   *South   West   North   East*
♡ J 7 3   4 ♠   all pass
◇ A
♣ 5

West leads the king of diamonds against your four spade contract. How do you plan the play?

That's a rather suitable dummy and your prospects of success are very good. You must make at least seven trumps and the two minor suit aces bring the tally up to nine tricks. There are several different ways of trying for the tenth trick. You could play on clubs, either finessing directly or taking a ruffing finesse on the second round. You could hope for either the ace or the queen of hearts to be favourably placed, or failing that you might be able to ruff the third round of hearts in dummy. And of course it may not be necessary for you to lose a trump trick. You could drop a singleton king or take a successful trump finesse.

It is hard to choose between these different lines of play, all of which seem to have some risk attached. Can you find a completely safe method of making ten tricks?

The correct play is to cross to the ace of clubs at trick two and lead the five of hearts from dummy. If East wins this trick it will establish an eventual heart winner for you, while if West captures your knave with the queen he will be unable to stop you ruffing a heart in dummy. He might lead away from K x x in trumps once, but he cannot do it twice except at the cost of his trump trick.

This attractive safety play was made by World Champion Belladonna of Italy in the 1965 European Championships at Ostend.

♠ K J 7 4
♡ J 9 2
◇ 8 6 5
♣ J 7 5

North-South game

	South	West	North	East
	2 ♡	3 ◇	—	4 ◇
	4 ♡	5 ◇	5 ♡	all pass

♠ A 9 3
♡ A K 10 8 7 6 4
◇ —
♣ A 10 6

West leads the ace of diamonds against your five heart contract. You ruff and play the ace of hearts, on which West drops the queen and East the three. How should you continue?

The enemy have pushed you rather high but there is no need for undue alarm. You have ten top tricks and a good chance of developing the eleventh. The spade holding is particularly promising. After drawing another round of trumps you could lead the three of spades to dummy's king, return the four to your ace and lead a third round. This will succeed if either defender has a singleton or doubleton honour card, if the suit breaks 3–3 (perhaps unlikely on the bidding), and if West has length in spades. This play may fail if East has four or more spades with the queen and ten, however, so perhaps you should look for something better.

There is in fact a completely safe way of making your contract. You should win the second round of trumps in dummy, ruff a diamond, and then play the ace and king of spades. You continue by leading dummy's last diamond and discarding your nine of spades on it.

The defender who wins this trick will be helpless. A spade lead from either side of the table will assure you of a third trick in the suit, while a diamond return will give you a ruff and discard. A club lead from West will give you two tricks in the suit, and a club through from East will leave his partner end-played and unhappy.

GOOD AND BAD BREAKS

♠ A 9 3
♡ A K 10 7 6 3　　　　　　*Love all*
♢ —
♣ 9 8 5 2

West	North	East	South
—	1 ♡	2 ♢	2 ♠
—	3 ♢	—	3 NT
—	5 ♣	—	6 ♠
all pass			

♠ K J 10 7 4
♡ Q
♢ Q 8 4
♣ A 10 7 3

Your partner is a complete stranger to you, and you have no premonition of disaster until dummy hits the table and you see that it is roughly an ace and a trump underweight. To bid like this the man must be a millionaire!

West's knave of diamonds leers at you from the table. How should you plan the play?

There would be problems enough in a contract of four spades, let alone six. At first glance it seems quite impossible to make the slam. Even a 3–3 heart break will not help you, since there is no way of making all eight of your trumps separately. Can there be any other method of gathering up twelve tricks?

In fact there is just one distribution of the major suits that will give you a chance. West must have queen and one other spade and four small hearts, leaving East with three spades and knave and another heart. Only on this layout will it be possible for you to get enough discards from the heart suit to scramble home.

You will need strong nerves for you have to make a hair-raising sequence of plays. After ruffing the first trick in dummy you should play a heart to your queen. You must now burn your boats by cashing the ace of clubs, for if you do not East may discard clubs on the hearts and eventually get a club ruff. At trick four you should lead a small trump to the table, finessing dummy's nine if West plays low. Next comes the ace of hearts from dummy and if East drops the knave you are almost there. You can discard a diamond on this trick, but when you continue hearts from dummy you must throw clubs, retaining a diamond in your hand. If East ruffs in on the third or fourth round of hearts you will

109

over-ruff, draw the two outstanding trumps by leading to dummy's ace, and finish the hearts. If East ruffs in on the fifth round you must over-ruff with the king of course.

Finally, if East hangs on to his trumps you will discard your last club on the fifth round of hearts. West can ruff this trick with his queen but, having no more trumps, he will be unable to stop you ruffing your last diamond in dummy.

The distribution you have to play for is shown below, and if you succeed in bringing home the slam you will not be entitled to complain about bad luck for at least six months.

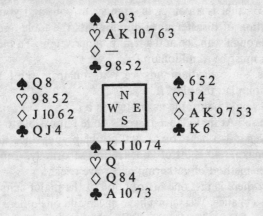

♠ A 9 3
♥ A K 10 7 6 3
♦ —
♣ 9 8 5 2

♠ Q 8
♥ 9 8 5 2
♦ J 10 6 2
♣ Q J 4

♠ 6 5 2
♥ J 4
♦ A K 9 7 5 3
♣ K 6

♠ K J 10 7 4
♥ Q
♦ Q 8 4
♣ A 10 7 3

CHAPTER 6

Backing the Favourite

When there is no way of making certain of the contract, the good player tries to select the line of play that offers the best chance of success. The declarer who has some knowledge of probabilities has an advantage here, since he is in a position to make an informed choice between two or more possible lines of play.

This does not mean that you have to delve deeply into probability theory, which for the non-mathematician has some baffling aspects. If Bayes sounds to you like a manufacturer of aspirins by all means continue in that happy belief. All that the practical bridge player needs is sufficient mathematical awareness to realize that if East has four cards in a suit and West two, any specific card in the suit is twice as likely to be with East as with West. The rest can be memorized.

The most important thing to know is how your suits are going to break. Every reader will be familiar with the percentage table showing the probable division of any number of outstanding cards in a given suit. For convenience the table is set out overleaf.

BACKING THE FAVOURITE

Cards Outstanding	Break	Probability %	Number of possible combinations
2	1–1	52	2
	2–0 & 0–2	48	(1 + 1) 2
3	2–1 & 1–2	78	(3 + 3) 6
	3–0 & 0–3	22	(1 + 1) 2
4	2–2	40·7	6
	3–1 & 1–3	49·7	(4 + 4) 8
	4–0 & 0–4	9·6	(1 + 1) 2
5	3–2 & 2–3	67·8	(10 + 10) 20
	4–1 & 1–4	28·3	(5 + 5) 10
	5–0 & 0–5	3·9	(1 + 1) 2
6	3–3	35·5	20
	4–2 & 2–4	48·4	(15 + 15) 30
	5–1 & 1–5	14·5	(6 + 6) 12
	6–0 & 0–6	1·5	(1 + 1) 2
7	4–3 & 3–4	62·2	(35 + 35) 70
	5–2 & 2–5	30·5	(21 + 21) 42
	6–1 & 1–6	6·8	(7 + 7) 14
	7–0 & 0–7	·5	(1 + 1) 2
8	4–4	32·7	70
	5–3 & 3–5	47·1	(56 + 56) 112
	6–2 & 2–6	17·1	(28 + 28) 56
	7–1 & 1–7	2·9	(8 + 8) 16
	8–0 & 0–8	·2	(1 + 1) 2

Anyone interested in checking the validity of the table can do so by applying the *nCr* formula. First calculate the number of possible hands the opponents can hold with their twenty-six known cards. This is given by the equation

$$26^c13 = \frac{26!}{13! \times 13!} = 10,400,600.$$ Now work out the number of

possible hands West can hold containing, say, two of the six outstanding trumps (and therefore eleven of the twenty non-trumps). The answer is $\dfrac{6!}{4! \times 2!} \times \dfrac{20!}{11! \times 9!} = 2{,}519{,}400$. Dividing this by 10,400,600 we get a percentage figure of 24·2, which agrees with the probability of the 2–4 break shown in the table.

Such calculations are too complicated to make at the bridge table, of course, so it will be helpful if you can commit the probability figures for the common breaks to memory.

It can be useful to know the number of possible combinations within each particular division of the outstanding cards when you wish to work out the chances of an opponent having some specific holding. For example, when there are five outstanding trumps the probability of East holding any specific doubleton (QJ, say) can be calculated as $\dfrac{67\cdot8 \%}{20} = 3\cdot4$ per cent.

Percentage plays for handling different card combinations have been fully explained by other writers and I do not propose to cover the same ground. A word of warning may be in order, however. The application of mathematical formulae to the play of the cards is a cold-blooded business which can be justified only when there is no other indication of the best line of play. The correct percentage play for a given combination of cards considered in isolation may be quite the wrong play for the hand as a whole. All available inferences from the bidding and play, and the human idiosyncrasies of the opponents should first be taken into account. An ounce of inference is worth a pound of percentage any day.

Furthermore, the odds on any particular division of the opponents' cards do not remain constant throughout the play of the hand. Although the probabilities calculated before the deal remain unaltered, the fresh information that comes to light during the course of play eliminates certain distributions as impossible. This enables us to express the ratio of the probabilities of holdings that are still possible in a new percentage figure. When we obtain a complete count of the hand probability gives way to certainty as regards distribution, and it is easy to calculate the chances of either opponent having a particular card.

BACKING THE FAVOURITE

Here is an elementary exercise in percentage play.

♠ K Q 4
♡ A 8 7   *Game all*
◇ 10 7 5 2
♣ 6 5 3   *South*   *North*
                 1 ♣   1 NT
                 2 ◇   2 ♡
♠ —   2 ♠   3 ♠
♡ K Q 6   5 ♣   —
◇ A K Q 4
♣ Q 10 8 7 4 2

West leads the knave of spades against your five club contract. You put up the queen from dummy, East plays the ace and you ruff. How should you continue?

The problem is to avoid three losers when trumps are 3–1, bearing in mind that you can only lead once from the table. The lead of a small club from hand followed by a lead from dummy on the second round will succeed if West has the single ace or king. The alternative of the queen of clubs at trick two and then a lead from dummy will gain only when West has the single knave, so this is an inferior play.

The correct lead of a low club has a total probability of success of 53·1 per cent (40·7 per cent for the 2–2 break plus half of the 24·8 per cent chance of a singleton with West) against 46·9 per cent for the lead of the queen. Substitute the nine for a small club in your hand or dummy's, however, and the lead of the queen would be equally good for it would then gain when either East or West had a singleton knave.

Finally, note that the percentage play of the low club is valid only because you have no indication as to where the opposing honour cards lie. If East had opened the bidding with one spade the lead of a low club would be quite wrong. East would be marked with the ace and king of clubs and your best chance would be to lead the queen.

♠ K 8 7 6 2
♡ A 9 7 4 2   *Game all*
♢ 3
♣ K 5   South   North
                           2 ♢   2 ♠
♠ A 5   4 ♢   4 ♡
♡ 3   4 NT   5 ♢
♢ A K Q J 10 6 4   5 NT   6 ♡
♣ A 8 4   7 ♢   —

West leads the seven of clubs against your grand slam contract. How do you plan the play?

You can count twelve tricks on top. The thirteenth could perhaps be made by ruffing your third club in dummy, or possibly by playing to establish dummy's fifth spade. The decision has to be taken immediately, for if you are going to try to set up the spade suit you will need to preserve dummy's king of clubs for later use as an entry card.

Probability is the only guide here. To play for a club ruff risks defeat when the clubs divide 6–2 or 7–1, which will happen 20 per cent of the time. Even if you successfully negotiate a club ruff you will still have to find a way back to your hand before you can draw trumps. The safest route back is by way of a spade to your ace, but that still risks the 1·5 per cent chance of either opponent being void in the suit. The total chance of success for the club ruff plan is thus 78·8 per cent.

The better line is to rely on the spades. Win the first trick with the ace of clubs and take as many rounds of trumps as are necessary, discarding hearts from dummy. By playing on spades you will now make your contract if the suit breaks 3–3 or 4–2, an 84 per cent chance. All will not necessarily be lost even if East shows out on the second round of spades. The chance of a double squeeze increases your overall probability of success to about 85 per cent.

♠ 7 6 2
♡ K 10 5
◇ A Q 8 7 4 2   *North-South game*
♣ 5

	South	North
	1 ♣	1 ◇
	1 NT	3 NT

♠ K 8 5 4
♡ A Q 3
◇ K
♣ A 9 8 6 3

West leads the queen of spades against your contract of three no trumps. East wins with the ace and returns the three, which you take with the king. How should you continue?

The contract will be simple if the diamonds break 3–3, but that is only a 35·5 per cent chance. The problem is how to augment your chances in the more likely (48·4 per cent) event of a 4–2 diamond split.

One way that suggests itself is to overtake the king of diamonds with dummy's ace and continue with the queen and the eight. This method will still win nine tricks if diamonds break evenly and will also succeed in the 4–2 breaks where the doubleton is J 10, J 9, or 10 9. The play has a 45·2 per cent chance of success, but this will reduce to 40·4 per cent if West plays a low diamond when you lead the king.

The other method is to cash the king of diamonds and then lead your small heart, finessing dummy's ten if West plays low. It is hard to assess the chances of this line since there is a human factor involved. If you can be sure that West is too unimaginative to play the knave of hearts if he has it, the odds are as good as 59·7 per cent. If West is a world champion, on the other hand, your chances will not be much higher than the 35·5 per cent of the 3–3 diamond break.

Against most defenders the proper course is to see what happens when you play the king of diamonds. If West plays the knave, ten or nine you should overtake in dummy, but if West plays low you should play low in dummy and attempt the heart finesse.

BACKING THE FAVOURITE

♠ 6
♡ A J 8 5 4 3
◇ Q J 7 2   *Love all*
♣ 7 4

	South	West	North	East
♠ A 5 2	1 ◇	—	1 ♡	1 ♠
♡ 9 6	2 ◇	2 ♠	4 ◇	—
◇ A 10 9 8 6 3	5 ◇	all pass		
♣ A 6				

West leads the four of spades against your five diamond contract, East plays the king and you win with the ace. How should you continue?

The diamond finesse gives you little more than a straight 50 per cent chance, for if it loses West is almost certain to switch to clubs and you will lose three tricks.

A better percentage can be obtained by combining the chances in the red suits in the optimum way. At trick two you should lead the six of hearts to dummy's ace, return to the ace of diamonds, and then lead the nine of hearts. This method will succeed when the king of diamonds is single (26 per cent) and fail when the diamonds break 3–0 (22 per cent). In the remaining 52 per cent zone where the diamonds are 2–1 and the king does not drop, you will be able to get your club loser away whenever West has three hearts (33·9 per cent), doubleton king and queen of hearts (3·4 per cent), and when East has the singleton king or queen of hearts (5·7 per cent). When the king of diamonds is with East you will also succeed if West has any other heart doubleton (14·4 per cent) or the singleton king, queen or ten of hearts (3·6 per cent). The total probability of these chances adds up to 57·7 per cent.

Those are the theoretical odds. The real ones are somewhat better, for if West has four hearts headed by the king and queen it is very likely that he will split his honours at trick two.

117

♠ A 8 6
♡ 9 2
◇ 7 6 4 3
♣ A J 6 5

♠ 4 3
♡ A K
◇ A K 5
♣ Q 10 9 8 4 2

Love all

South	North
1 ♣	3 ♣
5 ♣	

West leads the queen of hearts against your five club contract. How should you proceed?

Three lines of play suggest themselves and we had better examine each in turn. The first is the straightforward club finesse with a 50 per cent chance of success. Alternatively you could play a club to the ace and if the king does not drop continue with ace, king and another diamond. This succeeds if the club king is bare and in the other 2–1 club breaks when diamonds are 3–3. The total percentage is 44·5—clearly not good enough.

The third method is to play on diamonds before touching clubs. If diamonds prove to be 3–3 you can win the spade return, cash the ace of clubs and take a spade discard on the thirteenth diamond, while if diamonds are 4–2 you can always fall back on the club finesse. This method will fail when diamonds break worse than 4–2 (unless East has a freak hand with twelve or thirteen major suit cards). The total probability of success for the immediate diamond play is 52 per cent.

This appears to be slightly superior to the direct club finesse, but there is another factor to take into account. When the odds are close, preference should be given to the line of play that gives the defenders a chance to go wrong. If the club finesse loses it is by no means certain that a spade will come back. East may be tempted to lead a diamond up to dummy's weakness, and that gives you an additional chance. If you estimate that East will fail to find the spade return as little as a quarter of the time, the club finesse still beats the immediate diamond play by 2½ per cent.

BACKING THE FAVOURITE

```
♠ A K 9
♡ K 7 6 3 2          Love all
♦ 9 4
♣ 8 5 4          South   North
                  2 ♡     3 ♡
♠ 4 2             4 ♣     4 ♠
♡ A Q J 10 5      5 ♦     5 ♠
♦ A Q             6 ♡     —
♣ A Q J 7
```

West leads the queen of spades against your heart slam and East plays the six under dummy's ace. Both opponents follow when you play a heart to your ace. How should you continue?

This is a pretty good slam to be in. There is a 76 per cent chance that one of the minor suit finesses will be right, but of course you can do better than that. If the clubs break 3–3 the diamond finesse will be unnecessary. By drawing the last trump with dummy's king and then finessing clubs you will have a probability of success of 84·5 per cent.

But the best percentage is obtained by playing on elimination lines. At trick three you should lead a spade to dummy's king and ruff the nine of spades with a high trump. Now cash the ace of clubs, lead a high trump to dummy's king and return a club. If your knave wins this trick you can return to dummy by way of the seven of trumps to lead another club. This play will succeed if the king of clubs is with East, or if the clubs break 3–3, or if West has a singleton or doubleton king. If all these chances fail you can still ruff the fourth round of clubs and try the diamond finesse, which incidentally is better than a 50–50 shot when West is marked with four or five clubs. In playing off the king of spades and the ace of clubs before drawing the last trump you are running a slight risk of an enemy ruff, but this is more than offset by the other favourable chances. The total probability of success for this line of play is as good as 89 per cent.

♠ A 8 4 3
♡ 5   *Game all*
♦ Q 6 3
♣ A K J 10 6   *South*   *North*
                              2 ♡   3 ♣
                              3 ♡   3 ♠
♠ 10 9 5 2   4 ♠   5 ♣
♡ A K Q 7 4 2   5 ♦   6 ♡
♦ A K 7
♣ —

West leads the king of spades against your six heart contract.
You put on dummy's ace and East follows with the seven. How
should you continue?

That was an unfriendly lead. An attack in any other suit would
have left you with much better chances. But there are quite a
number of lines of play to consider as it is.

You could bank on the hearts breaking evenly and draw trumps
straight away. If the trumps prove to be 4–2 you will have the
slight additional chance of finding either defender with a doubleton queen of clubs. Total chance of success is a not very robust
37·6 per cent.

Alternatively you could try to make something of the clubs
before drawing trumps. If you play off the ace and king of clubs,
discarding spades from your hand, and then ruff a third round of
clubs you will succeed in the 4–2 trump breaks when the clubs are
5–3 with the queen in the shorter hand. You will also be all right
when you find the queen of clubs doubleton, but you will fail
when West has two small clubs even if trumps are 3–3 for on the
third round you will be over-ruffed. The total probability of success for this line of play is 42·8 per cent—an improvement.

What about ruffing a small club at trick two? This gives up the
chance of a doubleton queen of clubs except in the event of the
same hand having the doubleton trump. But this line will succeed
when trumps are 4–2 if either opponent has the queen and two

other clubs. It will also bring home the slam in all the 3–3 trump breaks and gives a total probability of success of 44·4 per cent. We appear to be improving our chances all the time.

There is just one other method to consider. You could play off the ace and king of clubs for immediate spade discards and continue with the knave of clubs, throwing your last spade if East plays low. In the 4–2 trump breaks you will have time to change your plan when either defender has the doubleton queen of clubs, and you will also succeed when East has three, four or five clubs including the queen. When East has six clubs including the queen this line will fail even if the trumps are 3–3. It will also fail in the 3–3 trump breaks when West has five clubs including the queen, or three or four clubs with the queen along with the rest of the spades, for then his partner will be able to uppercut a club or a spade return. Nevertheless, the total percentage increases to 47·3.

There is really not a great deal to choose between the last three lines of play and most declarers would find it impossible to make a comparison at the table.

The hand was played a few years ago in a Gold Cup semi-final match between Harrison-Gray and Leckie. The Scottish pair duly reached six hearts on the North-South cards and John MacLaren found himself faced with the problem of making the contract on the lead of the king of spades.

Whether by actuarial instinct or by some other means, MacLaren selected the best line of play by leading the ace and king of clubs and running the knave. But the story has no happy ending for Scottish readers. West had five clubs to the queen *and* four spades, so he actually had a choice of suits to lead for his partner's uppercut.

In the other room the inferior contract of six no trumps was reached. When the hearts broke 3–3 the result was a big swing against Leckie's team, which goes to show that in bridge as in life virtue must often be its own reward.

♠ A Q 7 4
♡ 10 7 5 2
◇ K 8 5   *Game all*
♣ A 3

	South	North
	1 ♠	4 ◇
	6 ♠	—

♠ K J 10 9 6 5
♡ A J 6
◇ A Q 7
♣ 4

West leads the king of clubs against your contract of six spades and you win with dummy's ace. Both opponents follow suit when you play off the ace of spades. How should you continue?

It is clearly desirable to eliminate the side suits before tackling hearts, so you will prepare the ground by ruffing dummy's three of clubs, drawing the last trump with your king and taking three rounds of diamonds ending in dummy. Now we are down to the bare bones of the problem. What is the best way of handling the heart suit?

You could, for instance, play a heart to your ace and continue with a small heart. This method will fail when the hearts break 3–3, but will succeed when either opponent has a doubleton honour (nine out of the fifteen possible 4–2 combinations). It will succeed in one-third of the 5–1 breaks, and perhaps in rather more than half of the 6–0 breaks (when East shows out you will have time to change your plan, but if West is void in hearts you will fail unless East comes to your rescue by splitting his honours).

An alternative is to lead a small heart to your knave, playing low in dummy on West's forced heart return. This will gain in 20 per cent of the 3–3 breaks (when East has both honours) and in the 4–2 breaks where East has a doubleton honour or both honours. It will also succeed in the 6–0 breaks, and in the 5–1 breaks when East has both honours, when either defender has a singleton honour and when East has the singleton eight or nine.

A third possibility is to lead a small heart to your knave and put up the ten from dummy on the second round. This method will succeed in the 3–3 breaks when both honours are together (40 per cent), and in seven of the fifteen possible 4–2 combinations plus all the 5–1 and 6–0 breaks.

Finally, you could lead the ten of hearts from dummy and try to run it. If East covered you would win with the ace, go back to dummy in trumps and lead another heart, putting up the knave if East plays low. This line will fail if hearts are 3–3 with the honours divided or if East has a singleton or doubleton honour.

With so many lines of play to choose from it may be helpful to set out the percentage odds in tabular form.

Break	Heart ace	Heart to J, then duck in dummy	Heart to J, then ten from dummy	Heart ten
	%	%	%	%
3–3	0	7·1	14·2	14·2
4–2	29·1	25·7	22·6	35·5
5–1	4·8	12·1	14·5	12·1
6–0	1·0	1·5	1·5	1·5
Total	34·9	46·4	52·8	63·3

As you can see, the lead of the ten of hearts is an easy winner in the percentage stakes. The true probability is rather higher than the 63·3 per cent shown because of the chance of a slip in defence. With three hearts to an honour East might fail to cover dummy's ten, in which case you will make your contract and West rude remarks.

♠ Q 4
♡ K Q 5
◇ A 8 7 2   *Game all*
♣ A K Q 6
                   North   South
♠ A J 10 2   2 NT   3 ♡
♡ A J 10 7 4   4 ♣   4 ♠
◇ 5   5 ◇   6 ♡
♣ 7 5 4

West leads the king of diamonds against your six heart contract,
you win with dummy's ace and East follows with the three.
Dummy's high cards fit your hand nicely without any awkward
duplication. The contract looks like a cake-walk until East discards
a spade on dummy's king of hearts. How should you continue?

The vicious five-nil trump break certainly complicates matters.
It looks as though the success of your slam will now depend on
the spade finesse being right, for you are sure to be forced in
diamonds if West gets in. The spade finesse is quite a lot better
than an even chance, of course. You know that West started with
five hearts and it is reasonable to assume that he has the queen of
diamonds to back up his king. That leaves just six unknown cards
in West's hand against eleven in East's. The odds are therefore
eleven to six that the king of spades is with East, giving a percentage of 64·7 for the straightforward play of drawing trumps,
entering dummy with a club and finessing in spades.

Since nobody likes to rely entirely upon a finesse it is worth
while looking to see if there is any chance at all when the king of
spades is wrong. You can, in fact, increase your total chances considerably by taking the spade finesse before drawing any more
trumps. The proper play at trick three is to lead the queen of
spades and run it if East plays low. If West wins with the king you can
ruff the diamond return, play two rounds of clubs and switch back
to spades. Provided that West has at least two cards in both black
suits you will make your slam. If West declines to ruff the third

or fourth round of spades you will simply discard dummy's clubs, making your twelfth trick by ruffing your third club on the table.

If your queen of spades wins the third trick, the safe way to continue is by cashing the ace and king of clubs. Should West ruff you will be able to trump the diamond return and draw trumps, the last round of which will squeeze East in clubs and spades. In the case where West follows to two rounds of clubs you can take a further spade finesse, secure in the knowledge that your slam cannot fail.

The danger of repeating the spade finesse before cashing two top clubs is that West could be playing a deep game with a hand like: ♠ K x x, ♡ 9 8 6 3 2, ◇ K Q x, ♣ x x. He would win the second spade and force you in diamonds and now you would have a communication problem incapable of solution. There would be no way of cashing two clubs and getting back to hand to run the spades without allowing West to make a trump trick.

When East has the king of spades the only occasion on which the immediate spade finesse will lose is when West is void in the suit and has four or more clubs. Then you will be a trick short with no hope of a squeeze. This holding of West's has a frequency of $2\frac{1}{4}$ per cent, which reduces your chances when the spade finesse is right from 64·7 per cent to 63·2 per cent.

However, your extra chances when the king of spades is wrong are quite substantial. Assuming West to have the king of spades and the king and queen of diamonds along with his five hearts there is still a 55·5 per cent chance that his remaining five cards include at least one more spade and two or more clubs. This increases the total probability of success for the recommended line of play to a useful 82·8 per cent.

♠ K 8 3
♡ J 7 6
◇ 10 9 6   *North-South game*
♣ K J 10 3   *West*   *North*   *East*   *South*
                      1 ◇   —   2 ◇   Double
♠ Q 10 7 5 4   3 ◇   Double   —   3 ♠
♡ A Q 10 9   —   4 ♠   all pass
◇ 5
♣ A Q 7

West starts with the two top diamonds against your four spade contract. After ruffing the second trick how should you continue?

Considering the spade suit in isolation, the normal percentage play is to lead low to the king and finesse the ten on the way back. But can that be the correct play in this case? There is really a problem within a problem here. The first concerns card-placing. It is likely from the bidding that East will have one of the outstanding high cards, either the ace of spades or the king of hearts. If it is the latter you will have no trouble on a normal 3–2 trump break, for you can afford to lose two trump tricks. If trumps are 4–1 you are unlikely to make this contract anyway.

The dangerous situation is when West has the king of hearts and East the ace of spades, and you must give yourself the best chance of losing only one trump trick if this is the case.

The proper play is to lead the seven of clubs to dummy's ten and return a low spade to your queen. If the queen wins you should play low in dummy on the next round unless West produces the knave.

On the assumption that the ace of spades is with East, the recommended play wins in 70 per cent of the 3–2 spade breaks (when East has A J, A x or A x x). The inferior play of a low spade to the king and a second round finesse of the ten wins in only 40 per cent of the 3–2 breaks (when East has A J or A J x).

BACKING THE FAVOURITE

♠ A J 7 4 3
♡ 9 4 3
◇ A Q 9   *North-South game*
♣ J 6
                 South   *North*
                 2 ♡   2 ♠
♠ 6   3 ♡   4 ◇
♡ A K Q J 8 5 2 4 ♡   5 ♡
◇ 5 4   6 ♣   6 ♡
♣ A Q 8

West leads the six of hearts against your slam contract and East contributes the seven. How do you plan the play?

At worst the slam depends on one of two finesses, which gives you a good 74 per cent chance of success. After drawing the outstanding trump, however, you should not neglect the opportunity of investigating the spade position by leading to the ace and ruffing the second round. The extra $1\frac{1}{2}$ per cent chance of either defender having the king and queen doubleton in spades increases your overall percentage to 74·4.

If either opponent shows out on the first or second round of spades you will have to play for one of the minor suit finesses being right, but if both follow to two rounds you can get better odds by playing to set up dummy's fifth spade.

At trick five you should lead the queen of clubs from hand. If East wins he will be unable to attack diamonds, and you will have enough entries in dummy to establish the fifth spade if the suit breaks 4–3 while still retaining the chance of the diamond finesse if spades break badly. If West takes your queen of clubs he will probably return a diamond, thereby removing one of your options. Your best chance will be to play the ace and rely on the 4–3 spade break.

The total probability of success for this line of play is 76·6 per cent plus the chance of a defensive error by West. If he fails to return a diamond it gives you an extra 7 per cent.

BACKING THE FAVOURITE

♠ A 8 7 6
♡ A 9 3   *North-South game*
◇ 10 7
♣ A Q 6 4

West	North	East	South
1 NT*	Double	—	2 NT
—	3 ♠	—	3 NT
all pass			

♠ K
♡ K 10 5 4
◇ Q 9 8 4
♣ J 10 8 2

12– 14 points

West leads the knave of spades against your three no trump contract and East follows with the five. Your knave of clubs is covered by the king and ace, both opponents follow to the club queen and East discards a diamond on the third round. How should you continue?

Taking the heart suit in isolation, the correct percentage play is to finesse the nine on the first round, following with the ace and (if West doesn't show out) the king. This has a 75 per cent chance of success, against 71·8 per cent for leading to the ace and finessing the ten and 70·2 per cent for leading to the ace and back to the king. But the finessing plays gain their advantage in the 5–1 and 6–0 breaks, which are clearly impossible here. On the bidding West must have more than one heart, while if he had five he would surely have led the suit. When we rule out the wilder breaks the probabilities of the 3–3 and 4–2 splits become 42·3 per cent and 57·7 per cent respectively.

A count of points is of little help. West could have both heart honours or neither, and there is no indication as to which defender is more likely to have a doubleton. Nowadays a holding such as J x in a major suit appears to be an incentive rather than a bar to bidding no trumps.

Falling back on probabilities we see that cashing the ace and king first will gain in eighteen of the thirty possible 4–2 and 2–4 distributions, while the other methods both succeed in sixteen cases. That gives a total probability of success of 76·9 per cent for playing off the top hearts, and 73·1 per cent for the finessing plays.

BACKING THE FAVOURITE

♠ 9 6 4 3
♡ 6 5
♢ Q 10 8 3   *Game all*
♣ 8 7 4
                    South   *North*
♠ A K 2   2 ♣   2 ♢
♡ A K Q   3 NT   —
♢ K J 9
♣ A J 5 2

West leads the ten of hearts against your three no trump contract and East plays the four. How do you plan your play?

There are six top tricks and you can easily develop two more in diamonds. It is unlikely that diamonds will provide the ninth trick, for the opponents will hold up the ace until the third round if they possibly can. The ninth trick will have to be developed in either spades or clubs.

Suppose you play off three rounds of spades. This will succeed when the spades break 3–3, and also when East has the doubleton Q J, Q 10, or J 10 in the suit. If the spades break badly for you there will still be the chance of finding the ace of diamonds singleton or doubleton. The total probability of success for this line is 50·7 per cent.

Better odds can be obtained in the club suit however. At trick two you should lead the two of clubs from your hand, win the heart (or spade) return, and play the king of diamonds. If this holds the trick you must next cash the ace of clubs before leading the knave of diamonds and overtaking with dummy's queen. If the diamond ace still does not appear you go for your last chance by leading the club towards your knave. This line wins when the clubs break 3–3, when West has a singleton king or queen of clubs, when either opponent has king, queen doubleton, and when West started with the king or queen and one other club. It will also succeed if the ace of diamonds is singleton or doubleton, unless the opponent with the doubleton ace also started with five clubs including the two top honours. Total chances add up to 62·7 per cent.

129

♠ 10 8 6
♡ 8 4
♢ A K J 5 3
♣ 9 8 4

North-South game

South	North
2 ♠	3 ♢
3 ♠	4 ♠

♠ A K J 9 7 5
♡ A J
♢ 8 2
♣ A 7 2

West leads the king of hearts against your four spade contract. How do you plan the play?

The straightforward line of play would be to lay down the ace of spades and, if nothing startling happened, continue with the king. Should the queen fail to drop there would still be the chance of the diamond finesse or a 3–3 diamond break.

There is another way of tackling the hand which at first glance is not too obvious. That is to play off the top diamonds before touching trumps and ruff a third diamond with your knave of spades. You would be quite happy to see West over-ruff, but if he doesn't you can continue by leading a small trump from your hand, thus establishing two entries in dummy to bring in a long diamond trick. This method will succeed if the diamonds are 3–3 unless West has all four trumps. It will also succeed when the diamonds are 4–2 with the trumps no worse than 3–1. There are extra chances when the queen of diamonds drops on the first or second round, for then you can alter your plan and tackle the trumps. There is even a slight chance when West is void in diamonds, and the total probability of success comes to 81 per cent.

You will certainly get a round of applause if you make your contract by such a subtle and exotic play. But practical players will stick to the unsubtle method of bashing out the ace and king of trumps, for it gives them a percentage of no less than 85·5.

CHAPTER 7

Communications

To the beginner at bridge communications is a nightmare subject, associated with humiliation and despair. The learner repeatedly suffers the embarrassment of finding himself locked in the wrong hand, unable to reach the tricks that are rightfully his, forced to lead away from a tenace holding or make some other lead that is advantageous to his opponents. The effect of a number of painful experiences is cumulative, however, and the beginner gradually learns to exercise a little forethought and avoid the more obvious traps.

COMMUNICATIONS

The more experienced player has learned the use of the duck in establishing his long suits, and appreciates the value of the hold-up in preventing the defenders from setting up theirs. He has some acquaintance with blocking and unblocking plays, and, having been taught to count his entries, he no longer embarks on a line of play that is bound to leave him stranded in the wrong hand. By the time he is approaching expert status he is conscious of the need for fluidity at all times. In going from hand to hand he selects his small cards with care, unblocking automatically when the need arises in order to provide entries in the hand that most requires them. In the expert the quality of foresight is cultivated to a high degree, and this is apparent in the way in which he handles problems of communication. By looking ahead and considering the probable way in which the hand will develop he acquires an understanding of the difficulties that may arise. Having spotted a possible blockage or other source of danger, he is half-way towards finding a method of circumventing it.

Communication plays divide themselves naturally into two main groups. On the one hand you have the ducking plays in all their countless variations, the unblocking plays and the entry-making gambits, all plays aimed at facilitating declarer's communications by creating or preserving entries to his own or dummy's hand. The other group comprises the hold-up plays, blocking plays, avoidance plays, and entry-destroying coups, plays designed to harass the defenders' lines of communication by forcing them to take their entry cards before they are ready to use them.

The field is a vast one. It would be hard, in fact, to imagine a bridge hand in which communication play in some form or other is not used. Naturally it will not be possible to cover the entire range within the confines of this chapter. The problems here have been selected to illustrate some of the less familiar and more piquant aspects of the subject.

COMMUNICATIONS

♠ 3 2
♡ 9 6 3
♢ A K Q J 7 6 5
♣ 7

Love all

	South	North
♠ K J 10 4	1 ♣	1 ♢
♡ K Q 8 2	1 ♡	3 ♢
♢ 3	3 NT	—
♣ K Q 10 6		

West leads the nine of spades against your three no trump contract. East wins with the ace and returns the five of spades. How do you plan the play?

There seems to be a conflict of evidence here. West's lead of the nine suggests that he is short in spades, but if East has the queen why didn't he switch? He would be able to count your nine tricks and his proper course would be to switch to hearts or clubs in the hope that the defence could take five tricks before you got going.

This is really a very simple hand. Only a greedy or a thoughtless declarer will finesse in spades on the second trick. The danger is that West may win and shoot back a diamond, severing your only line of communication with dummy. You would then have to run the diamond suit which would inflict a suicide squeeze on your own hand. Whether you cashed all seven diamonds or left one or more in dummy you would be unable to make more than eight tricks altogether.

At match-point pairs the problem would be more complicated, but at other forms of the game there can be no doubt about the proper course of action. You should win the second trick with the king of spades and establish your ninth trick before touching the diamonds by leading the king of hearts. This keeps open a channel of communication between the hands, and the opponents can make no more than two spade tricks, one heart and one club.

133

COMMUNICATIONS

♠ 7 6 3
♡ A 5 3
◇ 8 2
♣ Q J 8 4 2

North-South game

♠ A K 2
♡ K 10 7
◇ A K J 4
♣ K 9 5

South	North
2 NT	3 NT

West leads the queen of spades against your three no trump contract. How do you play?

There is no case for holding up in spades, so you win the first trick with your king. Now the question is how to tackle the clubs so as to be sure of three tricks from the suit. With those cards there are always three eventual winners, but the fact that dummy has only one outside entry should make you approach the problem with care.

You will always be sure of an overtrick when the clubs break 3–2, of course. You will also be all right when West has four or five clubs, provided that you do not block the suit by retaining the nine in your hand. The only situation that constitutes a serious threat to the safety of your contract is where East has four clubs to the ace and ten.

In handling honour combinations it is normal practice to maintain flexibility by leading first towards the hand which holds two honours, but that will not be good enough here. If you lead the nine of clubs to dummy's knave, both opponents playing small, and return a club to your king, your contract will be in jeopardy if West shows out on the second round.

The way to protect yourself against any eventuality is to lead the club king at the second trick. If this wins you can continue with the nine of clubs, putting on dummy's knave if West follows suit. When West shows out on the second round you will play small from dummy, forcing East to take his ten while you still have a club left to enable you to establish the suit.

♠ 8 7 2
♡ 10 8 4
◇ A Q 8 3   *East-West game*
♣ K Q 3

	West	North	East	South
			1 ♠	2 ♡
	2 ♠	3 ♡	—	4 ♡
	all pass			

♠ J 10
♡ K Q J 9 6 3
◇ 9
♣ A J 7 6

West leads the king of spades against your four heart contract. East overtakes with the ace and returns the eight of clubs. How do you plan the play?

You can count five trump tricks, four clubs and one diamond, making a healthy total of ten. The only danger is that one of the opponents may be able to ruff a club. But from the way the defence has gone it is apparent that this is a very real danger. Why do you think East overtook his partner's king of spades in order to lead a club? It must be because his eight of clubs is a singleton. No doubt he intends to win the first trump lead and put his partner in with the queen of spades to give him a club ruff. If that is the situation is there anything you can do about it?

Once you recognize the problem you are within sight of a solution. If you reflect for a moment on the bidding you will realize that East is almost bound to have the king of diamonds as well as the ace of hearts. In that case you will be able to defeat his plan by exchanging your spade loser for a diamond one. After winning the club lead in dummy you should lead out the ace of diamonds and continue with the queen, discarding your knave of spades when East produces the king. East will now be stuck on lead, unable to reach his partner's hand, and the danger of the club ruff will be averted.

This play has been aptly named the scissors coup, since it is designed for the sole purpose of snipping the defenders' line of communication.

COMMUNICATIONS

♠ 10 6
♡ 7
◇ A K Q
♣ A 10 8 7 6 5 3

North-South game

West	North	East	South
1 ♠	2 ♣	2 ♠	3 ♡
—	4 ♣	—	4 ♡
all pass			

♠ Q 2
♡ A K J 10 8 6 2
◇ J 10 3
♣ 4

West leads the knave of clubs against your four heart contract. You win with dummy's ace and East follows with the two. How should you continue?

East appears to have the king and queen of clubs, in which case West must have opened rather light and will surely have the queen of hearts as well as the two top spades. But that's all right. You can afford to lose two spades and a heart and still make your contract. Is there any danger that you might lose two heart tricks? There is certainly nothing you can do if West has all five outstanding hearts, but it would be sensible to take precautions in case he has four hearts and a singleton club.

There is no question of finessing in hearts, naturally, but the immediate play of ace, king and another would also be unsafe if West has something like ♠ A K x x x x, ♡ Q 9 x x, ◇ x x, ♣ J or ♠ A K J x x, ♡ Q 9 x x, ◇ x x x, ♣ J. With either of those holdings West could defeat you by taking his queen of hearts, cashing the two top spades, and putting you in dummy with a diamond lead. You would be unable to get back to your hand except by leading a club, and West would make a second trump trick.

This danger is averted easily enough by cashing a diamond at trick two, and then discarding dummy's two remaining diamonds on the second and third rounds of trumps. That leaves a clear line back to your hand whatever West may return.

COMMUNICATIONS

```
♠ A 7 5 4
♡ Q 3                    North-South game
♦ Q J 8 5
♣ K Q J        West    North    East    South
                                 1 ♠     Double
♠ 2             —       2 ♠      —       3 ♡
♡ A J 10 9 6    —       3 ♠      —       4 ♣
♦ K 10 3        —       4 ♡      all pass
♣ A 10 6 5
```

West leads the knave of spades against your four heart contract. How do you plan the play?

Perhaps you have underbid this one, for there is quite a good chance of twelve tricks. But since you did not bid the slam you need concern yourself only with the safest way of making ten tricks.

Leaving aside the wilder trump breaks, there can be danger only when West has the doubleton king of hearts. Then you will be forced in spades, and after drawing trumps you will be able to run only nine tricks before letting East in with the ace of diamonds to enjoy the rest of his spades.

Hold-up play might help if West has only two spades, but if you play low from dummy on the first trick you could look silly. Either opponent might switch to one of the minor suits and eventually obtain a ruff for the fourth defensive trick.

Although a hold-up is not practicable, the idea of trying to exhaust West's spades is sound. The proper way to effect it is to win the first trick and lead out the queen of diamonds. If this is allowed to hold you have your tenth trick and can switch to trumps. If East takes the ace of diamonds he will play a spade to force your hand. You can ruff, enter dummy with a club and take the heart finesse. Now if West wins he may well have no spade left to lead. Since you can afford to lose three tricks you don't mind if an opponent gets a ruff in either minor suit. And if the ace of diamonds turns up in the West hand after all, you can be quite sure that the trump finesse will work.

137

♠ A 10 7 4
♡ 10 6 4 3
◇ J 10 6
♣ 10 5

Love all

	South	North
	2 NT	3 ♣
	3 NT	—

♠ Q J 2
♡ A K J
◇ Q 9
♣ A Q J 7 6

West leads the two of diamonds against your three no trump contract. How do you plan the play?

If the lead is honest the diamonds are breaking luckily for you and you should make this contract unless both the spade and club finesses are wrong. But you will still have to handle your entries with care, for it is desirable to take the club finesse before the cramping effect of the opponents' long diamonds makes itself felt. You have nothing to lose and possibly a great deal to gain by putting up the ten or the knave from dummy on the first trick, unblocking with your queen if East produces an honour card.

The danger in playing low from dummy is that you may be permitted to win the first trick with your queen or nine. Then you would have to tackle the spades first, which could lead to trouble. East might win and return a diamond and you would discard, say, one club and the knave of hearts from your hand. On winning the heart return you would then have a nasty guess to make. You could either take your three spade tricks and rely on East having just K x in clubs, or you could overtake your knave of spades with dummy's ace and finesse clubs twice, hoping for one of the black suits to break 3–3.

It is not easy to foresee the ending in detail at the first trick, but you will not go wrong if you follow the general principle of trying to create entries in the hand most likely to need them.

♠ A J 7
♡ K 5 4
♢ J 4 2
♣ Q J 6 3

Game all

	South	North
	1 ♠	2 NT
	4 ♠	—

♠ Q 10 9 5 3 2
♡ J 6
♢ K 8
♣ A K 7

West leads the three of diamonds against your contract of four spades. How do you plan the play?

Five trumps, four clubs and a diamond add up to ten tricks all right, but if everything is wrong it is just possible that the defenders will take four tricks first. For that to happen a heart would have to be led by West, of course, and the only suit in which West might regain the lead is diamonds.

It is not very likely that West has underled the ace of diamonds. If he has you will not be able to stop him getting in to lead a heart through anyway, so you can forget about that possibility. What other diamond holding could he have? If he has led from the ten he will never be able to regain the lead if you play low from dummy, but this is rather a poor chance. A lead from four to the ten against a suit contract could hardly be classed as dynamic, and it is altogether more likely that West has led from the queen. East could have a hand like ♠ K x, ♡ A Q x x, ♢ A 10 x x, ♣ x x x. If you play a low diamond from dummy East may reason that you cannot be missing the king of diamonds on the bidding and put in the ten. When he later gets in with the king of spades he will be able to put his partner in by underleading the diamond ace, and a heart will inevitably come back.

To prevent this you should play dummy's knave of diamonds on the first trick. Whether East takes his ace or ducks, this blocking play ensures that West will not be on lead again.

COMMUNICATIONS

♠ A 10
♡ Q J 6
♢ K J 10 4
♣ A K 8 3

Love all

North	South
1 ♢	1 NT
2 NT	3 NT

♠ 9 6 3 2
♡ A 8 3
♢ Q 7
♣ Q 7 6 2

West leads the five of spades against your three no trump contract. How should you plan the play?

It would of course be needlessly risky to play the ten of spades on this trick. West would not lead low from K Q J x x. If West has five spades East is marked with a doubleton honour and the play of the spade ace will give the enemy communication trouble. East will be unable to unblock by throwing his honour card under the ace without setting up a second spade stopper in your hand.

Having won the first trick, how should you set about making your contract? On a normal 3–2 club break you will make nine tricks without much effort by playing on diamonds. But if the clubs are 4–1 you will need a second heart trick and will have to watch your timing. Playing on diamonds could result in defeat if East has the diamond ace and West the king of hearts. After taking his diamond ace East would cash his spade honour and lead a heart and that would be that.

In order to determine which of the red suits to tackle first it is necessary to know how the clubs are breaking, so at trick two you should lead a low club to your queen and return a club to dummy's king. If the clubs prove to be 4–1 you must next risk the heart finesse so as to knock out West's potential entry.

Of course you will suffer defeat if West has something like ♠ K J x x x, ♡ K x x, ♢ A x x x, ♣ x, but if that is the case there was never any play for your contract.

140

COMMUNICATIONS

♠ A K J
♡ 5 3 2
◇ Q J 8 6 5   *Game all*
♣ K Q
                    South   *North*
♠ Q   2 ♡   3 ♡
♡ A Q J 10 9 6   4 ♣   4 ♠
◇ A 7 4 2   5 ◇   6 ♡
♣ A 3

West leads the nine of spades against your six heart contract. How should you plan the play?

A successful finesse in either red suit will see you home, but with only two entries in dummy it is important to take the finesses in the right order. In a no trump contract you would take the diamond finesse first, for if it failed you would still have the two entries you might need for the heart finesse. In the heart slam, however, it would be too dangerous to tackle the diamonds before drawing trumps: someone might get a ruff. So after winning the first trick in dummy you should take an immediate trump finesse. If it loses you will be able to win the return, draw trumps and get back to dummy in clubs to try the diamond finesse.

If West shows out on the first round of trumps the position is the same as when the finesse fails. With no way of avoiding a trump loser, you must cede a trick to the heart king, draw trumps and eventually finesse in diamonds.

When the queen of hearts wins the second trick and West follows, however, you should not make the too ready assumption that the trump finesse is working. West could be holding off with K x x. To guard against this possibility you should, after leading a club to dummy, cash another top spade and throw your ace of clubs on it. Now a further trump lead will expose the situation. If East shows out you will play the ace of hearts and continue the suit, and West will have to put dummy on lead, enabling you to take the diamond finesse.

141

♠ K 9 7 4
♡ A Q 4 2
♢ 7 6   *Love all*
♣ K 9 3

South	West	North	East
1 NT	—	2 ♣	2 ♢
2 ♠	—	4 ♠	all pass

♠ J 10 8 2
♡ K 6 3
♢ K 3
♣ A Q 8 4

West leads the knave of diamonds against your four spade contract and East follows with the nine. How should you plan the play?

There is nothing wrong with this contract. Given a normal trump break you would expect to lose a diamond and two spade tricks at the most. Nevertheless there can be no excuse for careless play in this situation. East's play of the nine of diamonds should automatically arouse your suspicion. Could he have a special reason for not taking his ace of diamonds on the first round? It may be that he has a singleton in either hearts or clubs along with the ace, queen and another trump. In that case he will be planning to win the first trump lead and shoot back his singleton. Then on winning the second round of trumps he will be able to cross the table with a diamond lead to his partner's ten and get his ruff.

Fortunately, a simple counter to this plan is available. The proper play is to let the trumps wait and return a diamond at trick two. This is a less spectacular variation of the scissors coup, but it is just as effective in isolating the defenders from each other.

Of course it may be that East played the nine of diamonds on the first trick not with any deep plot in mind but just as a matter of sound defensive technique. Equally, it is technically correct for declarer to return the suit, even if he does not reason out the play from first principles.

COMMUNICATIONS

♠ A 7 5
♡ Q 9 4
◇ A 8 7
♣ A Q 9 6

North-South game

	West	North	East	South
	1 ♡	1 NT	—	3 ♠
	—	4 ♠	all pass	

♠ J 10 8 6 4 2
♡ K 6 3
◇ 5
♣ J 10 2

West leads the king of diamonds against your four spade contract. You win with dummy's ace and play off the ace of spades on which West drops the king. East takes the queen of spades on the next round, his partner throwing a small diamond, and switches to the eight of hearts. How do you play?

If this eight of hearts is a singleton East will get a ruff and your contract will then depend upon the position of the king of clubs. West is likely to have that card, but there is no certainty about it. If East has two hearts, on the other hand, you can make this contract even if the club finesse is wrong. There is, however, one important proviso. You must play the king of hearts on this trick. To play low could well prove fatal. West will insert the ten to force dummy's queen and, if East subsequently obtains the lead with the king of clubs, a further heart lead will defeat you.

The play of the king of hearts is an entry-destroying play designed to prevent West from enjoying more than one trick in his long suit. The position is perhaps easier to recognize in defence. When dummy has a suit headed by A J 10 and no outside entries and declarer leads the eight, the play of second hand high by the defender on declarer's left is a well-known manœuvre. It is not so often that the declarer is called upon to make this second hand high play, but you should be on the alert for occasions like this when it does turn up.

COMMUNICATIONS

♠ A 10 5
♡ Q 3
◇ J 7 5 4   *Game all*
♣ A 9 7 2

                    South   *North*
♠ 8 4   1 ♡   2 NT
♡ A J 10 8 7 5 2   4 ♡   —
◇ A 10
♣ 6 5

West leads the nine of diamonds against your four heart contract, East plays the queen and you win with the ace. How should you continue?

Ten tricks will be there for the taking even if the king of hearts is wrong provided that you can get one of your black losers away on dummy's knave of diamonds. But there may well be difficulty in communications in achieving this.

If you enter dummy with one of the black aces in order to finesse in trumps you will fail if West produces the king of hearts and attacks the other black suit, for then the opponents will be a tempo ahead.

What about returning diamonds straight away then? That will work out all right if West has three cards in the suit, but he may have only a doubleton, in which case you will again fail if the heart finesse is wrong.

To lead out ace and another trump will not be good enough if either defender has three trumps to the king, for a spade or club lead will leave you with no quick way back to your hand to draw the last trump.

The correct play is to lead a small trump from your hand at trick two. This maintains trump communications between the table and your hand and enables you to cope with almost any distribution. The exception is when either defender started with a singleton diamond and his partner with a singleton or doubleton king of hearts, for a second round diamond ruff will leave you without a tenth trick.

144

COMMUNICATIONS

♠ A 6
♡ Q 7 4
◇ A Q
♣ A Q 10 7 6 3

Game all

♠ K 3
♡ K 10 2
◇ J 6 4 3
♣ J 9 5 2

West	North	East	South
3 ♠	Double	—	3 NT
all pass			

West's lead of the queen of spades is not altogether unexpected. How do you plan the play?

Assuming, as you should, that the club finesse is wrong, you have only eight winners and will need to develop the ninth in either hearts or diamonds. Since the ace of hearts is the only entry that West can have for his long spades, it must be correct to try to knock it out at trick two before touching the clubs. If West does have the heart ace he will have to choose between using his entry prematurely and ceding your ninth trick straight away.

There are communication problems in your hand, however. What is the best way of attacking the hearts? To win the first trick in dummy and lead a heart to your king would not be safe, for West might have a doubleton ace and return the suit to set up three more heart tricks for his partner.

Nor is it satisfactory to win the first trick in your hand and lead a heart to dummy's queen. East could produce the ace and return a spade, which would leave you in an awkward position, wanting to finesse in clubs but unable to do so without releasing control of the heart suit.

The correct method of play is to win the first trick in dummy and lead the queen of hearts. This guarantees your contract on the one reasonable assumption that East has no more than two spades. If East wins and returns a heart you will finesse the ten, and no continuation of West's can hurt you.

♠ A K J 6
♡ 9 7 6 5
◇ —
♣ 9 8 6 4 3

North-South game

South	North
1 ◇	1 ♠
2 NT	3 NT

♠ 9 2
♡ A 10 4
◇ A K 10 7 3
♣ A Q 5

West leads the three of hearts against your three no trump contract, East plays the queen and you win with the ace. How should you continue?

With only six top tricks you will have to develop three more. No doubt you could set up another heart trick eventually, and there is a chance of an extra trick in spades, but you will still need the club finesse for your ninth trick. In that case why not rely on the club suit for all three extra tricks? It only needs a 3–2 break for this plan to work.

Dummy's diamond void gives you a tricky communication problem, however. If you cross to dummy in spades, take a successful club finesse, and continue with ace and another club there will be no way back to your hand to cash the diamond winners. After the queen of clubs wins you could of course continue with a small club, keeping the club ace as an entry for the diamonds, but this play exposes dummy's entry to attack. A spade lead from either defender would cut you off from the long clubs and hold you to seven or eight tricks.

The only solution is to conserve entries, both in your hand and in dummy's, like a miser. The correct play at trick two is a small club from hand. This play retains control of the situation no matter what the enemy may do. You will sooner or later get in to dummy with a spade, take the club finesse, cash the club ace and the top diamonds and then return to dummy in spades to cash the remaining clubs.

♠ Q 3
♡ A K Q 7
◇ A 9 7 6 2   *Game all*
♣ Q 10

	West	*North*	*East*	*South*
			1 ♣	1 ♠
♠ K J 9 8 6 5 2	2 ♣	3 ♣	—	3 ♠
♡ 6 5 4	—	4 ♠	all pass	
◇ 5 3				
♣ 7				

West leads the ten of trumps against your four spade contract. You cover with dummy's queen and East plays the four. How should you continue?

You have your ten tricks with six spades, three hearts and a diamond, but it looks as though East is up to some funny business again. If the trumps do not break evenly your contract could be in danger. East might have a hand like ♠ A x x, ♡ x, ◇ Q J x, ♣ A J x x x x, in which case he no doubt intends to win the second round of trumps and lead his singleton heart, pinning you on the table with no immediate way of getting back to your hand to draw the last trump. Whether you play clubs or diamonds West will win and give his partner a heart ruff.

Yes, it is another hand in which you have to break contact between defenders by means of the scissors coup. At trick two you should lead a club from the table. If the defenders then switch to hearts you can continue with a second round of trumps safe in the knowledge that you cannot be locked into dummy.

The best defence to your club lead will be the continuation of a second round of clubs at trick three. This variation offers you a further chance to go wrong by trying to draw trumps too soon, but you have two equally good counters available. You can either discard your losing diamond on the second round of clubs, or you can ruff and play out the ace and another diamond. Both methods ensure that you will have a means of access to your own hand after you have forced out the ace of trumps.

♠ Q 10
♡ A K Q 4
◇ 8 3
♣ Q J 9 5 2

North-South game

	West	North	East	South
	—	1 ♣	1 ♠	2 ◇
♠ A 9 8	—	2 ♡	—	2 NT
♡ 7 5	—	3 NT	all pass	
◇ A Q J 10 2				
♣ 10 6 4				

West leads the seven of spades against your contract of three no trumps, and dummy's ten is covered by East's knave. How do you plan the play?

Although your nine tricks appear to be there (counting two spades, three hearts and four diamonds), there may be some difficulty in taking them due to the weakness in communications. Could there possibly be an advantage in allowing East to hold the first trick? Only if East has six spades and just one outside entry, which must be rather against the odds. Besides, it could be dangerous to concede a tempo by holding off the first trick.

You could finesse twice in diamonds, of course. This will succeed when East has the king and one or two other diamonds, and possibly when the finesse is wrong if West can be persuaded to win on the first round.

However, there is a much better method of playing the hand which will make certain of your contract whenever the diamonds break no worse than 4–2. After winning the first trick you should lead the queen of diamonds from hand. If the defenders hold off you will continue with the ace and then the knave of diamonds, discarding the queen of spades from dummy. The jettison of the blocking spade will make it impossible for the defenders to press home their spade attack without allowing you to make an easy nine tricks. They will have to play on dummy's suits instead, and that will suit you nicely. Eventually you will establish three club tricks to add to your three hearts, two diamonds and a spade.

Note that you cannot afford to enter dummy with a heart at trick two in order to finesse once in diamonds. On winning the

third round of diamonds, the opponents would then be a tempo
ahead and might be able to establish a heart trick for themselves
before you could set up the clubs.

CHAPTER 8

Pressure Play

Although the subject matter of this chapter may be only of limited practical importance, it nevertheless forms the most fascinating and the most rewarding single area of study in the whole field of card play. The time is long past when the squeeze was the prerogative of the expert. Many first-class writers on both sides of the Atlantic have freely given away their secrets, and with the resulting general improvement in standards of play more enthusiasts are squeezing today than ever before. For all that, in bridge circles the possession of a comprehensive knowledge of squeeze technique remains a more significant status symbol than the ownership of, say, an expensive car or a second television set.

What is more, squeezes are great fun. Players who cannot be bothered to study squeeze play are undoubtedly missing the supreme thrill of this game of ours. For sheer mental exhilaration there is nothing to equal the satisfaction of carrying a deliberately planned squeeze to a successful conclusion. Psychologists may claim that there is a sadistic element in the enjoyment with which we watch the squirming of the defender under pressure, and from a moral point of view perhaps it is as well that we are not allowed to taste this pleasure too frequently.

What discourages many players from attempting to improve their acquaintance with squeeze technique is that it is necessary to work at the subject. There are many positions to learn and each has its own requirements as regards timing and the arrangement of entries and menaces. Card-playing ability on its own may not be enough to guide you through this maze, for it can be very difficult to work out the correct play from first principles. The player whose powers of analysis enable him to think his way through each problem as it arises is rare indeed. Where squeeze play is concerned recognition is more than half the battle, and the only way to be sure of recognizing the less familiar squeeze positions is to study example hands.

The complexity of the subject and the need to classify so many different types of squeeze compelled the early writers on squeeze play to adopt a vocabulary of their own. In doing so they displayed a degree of rugged individualism which, while admirable in itself, tended to complicate matters for their readers. It is only comparatively recently that there has been a move towards standardizing squeeze terminology.

I wonder if anyone reads Robert Rendel now. His little gem of a book, published in 1934, dealt competently with all the main types of squeeze and gave the readers of the day a very good two shillings' worth. But anyone tackling the book today would be well advised to have a quart of black coffee and a bottle of aspirins at his elbow. To dip into Rendel is to enter an Alice-Through-the-Looking-Glass world where all our terms of reference are overthrown. What we know today as a double squeeze is a 'compound triple squeeze' in Rendel's book. Our progressive or repeating triple squeeze is called a 'double squeeze', the guard squeeze is a 'triple squeeze', and the automatic squeeze on the opponent to the right of the squeeze card is an 'inverted squeeze'. It is all perfectly logical, but the point of view is outdated and unfamiliar.

Most of the serious writers on the squeeze have been very explicit in laying down the basic conditions that must obtain before a squeeze can operate, but they have shown a startling lack of uniformity in coining mnemonic aids. Reese kept it simple with MEST, which Brown transformed into a curious quadruped flowering upon a STEM, a notion that hardly seems biologically sound. Coffin preferred to remain alphabetical, or perhaps musical, with his EFG, while Love's BLUE introduced a touch of colour to the subject. Freehill, of course, outbid them all with MESPOT, which sounds for all the world like something out of a James Bond thriller (Middle European Society for the Propagation of Organized Terror?).

Having no wish to hasten the day when there will be a need for some mnemonic to help remember all the mnemonics, I am not going to inflict another group of initials on you. I shall assume that any reader who has not tossed this book in the waste-paper basket by now will be well aware of what is needed to make a squeeze function. If I do this I must also assume that you are quite familiar with the types of squeeze most commonly encountered—the simple single and double squeezes. The problems in this chapter will therefore deal in the main with situations that are rather more complex but still amenable to single dummy analysis at the bridge table.

♠ A K 5
♡ 10 7 4 2
◇ Q J 7 6
♣ J 10

Game all

South	North
2 NT	3 ♣
3 ◇	6 ◇
—	

♠ Q 7 6 3
♡ A K
◇ A K 5 3
♣ A 8 4

West leads the queen of hearts against your six diamond contract. Both opponents follow to the ace of diamonds and to the second high heart, but when you continue with a low diamond to dummy's queen East discards a club. How do you plan the play?

The 4–1 trump break makes it impossible to ruff both of dummy's hearts in your hand, but there are still some chances. The knave of hearts might fall on the third round, for instance, or the spades could break evenly. Say you play a heart from dummy and ruff with your small trump and both defenders follow but the knave does not appear. Now you play off the king of diamonds and East discards another club. You cross to the ace of spades in dummy and draw the last trump, on which East throws a third club. Naturally you discard a club yourself on this trick. What next?

Since West started with eight red cards to East's four, it is perhaps unlikely that the spades will break 3–3. Still, in order to remove ambiguity, it is correct to test the spades next. The manner in which you do this could be important, though. The proper method is a low spade to your queen and then a spade back to dummy's king. If East proves to have four spades you wish the lead to be in dummy after the tenth trick, for there is still a faint chance. At this stage everyone is down to three cards. If East has both the king and queen of clubs along with his master spade the lead of the ten of hearts—a losing squeeze-card—will force him to surrender.

♠ A 7 3
♡ Q 10 6 5
◇ 6 2
♣ A K J 5

♠ K 4
♡ K J 9 7 2
◇ 10 8 5 3
♣ 7 3

Love all

West	North	East	South
1 ◇	Double	1 ♠	2 ♡
2 ♣	3 ♡	—	4 ♡
all pass			

Against your four heart contract West starts with the ace of diamonds on which East plays the nine. West switches to the three of trumps, East plays the four and you win with the seven. You test West's nerves by leading the ten of diamonds, but after a little thought he plays low and East wins the trick with the knave. Annoyingly, East continues with the ace and another heart, on which West discards a diamond and a spade. Take it from there.

Since you have not been permitted to ruff both of your losing diamonds in dummy, the problem now is to locate the queen of clubs. There are, of course, two possible ways of tackling the club suit. On the bidding it is certainly likely that West has the queen, but it would be a pity to take a losing finesse and discover afterwards that East's queen could have been ruffed out.

Rather than risk an immediate club finesse you should first try to discover as much as possible about the opponents' distribution by playing off the two top spades and ruffing dummy's third spade in your hand. If West follows suit you will know that he began with only three clubs and you will have to rely on him for the queen. But if, as seems more probable on the bidding, West started with a 3–1–5–4 distribution, the third round of spades will bring irresistible pressure to bear upon him. You will establish your tenth trick by ruffing out whichever minor suit he unguards.

♠ K 10
♡ A K Q 3
♢ J 9 5 3
♣ Q 7 4

North-South game

North	South
1 ♡	1 ♠
1 NT	3 ♡
3 ♠	4 ♠

♠ A Q J 8 6
♡ 9 8 4
♢ 6 4
♣ K 6 2

West leads the ace of diamonds against your four spade contract and East encourages with the eight. West continues with the king and another diamond and you have to ruff East's ten. How should you continue?

If both major suits break 3–3 you are in the clear, but the odds are seven to one against that happening. When the trumps are 4–2 you will not be able to make your contract if East has the club ace, so you may as well assume that West has that card. If West has the long hearts as well there is a chance of a squeeze, but in order to reduce ambiguity in the possible squeeze ending it is desirable to play a round of clubs at an early stage. Since your hand has no entries outside the trump suit the proper play is a low club towards the queen at trick four. If the queen holds you can rattle off four rounds of spades and watch West's reactions.

♠ —
♡ A K Q 3
♢ —
♣ 7 4

♠ J
♡ 9 8 4
♢ —
♣ K 6

Suppose that on the third round of spades West has discarded a club and you have thrown dummy's knave of diamonds. The knave of spades now forces a further discard from West. You cannot be sure of reading the position correctly, of course. After West has discarded it may not be easy to tell whether he has bared his ace of clubs in order to keep four hearts or whether the hearts are breaking all the time. But West's wriggling, or his failure to wriggle, or the size of his club discard may give you a clue.

Note that this position does not conform to the usual squeeze rule that all declarer's cards except one should be winners. For all that it is one of the commonest of squeeze endings—the two-suit strip-squeeze.

Some confusion exists about the loser count in squeeze play and perhaps an attempt at clarification would be helpful. All the basic positions are one-loser squeezes. If the declarer has more than one loser in the combined hands he must rectify his loser count by conceding the required number of tricks before any squeeze can take place.

For a squeeze to be effective when the declarer has two or more losers there must always be some compensating factor. In the case of the strip-squeezes this is either a minor tenace in a defender's hand so that he is threatened with a throw-in, or, as in the last hand, an extension of the one card menace in declarer's or dummy's hand which compels the defender to keep a guard to his winner. If the defender has no exit cards in a third suit the strip-squeeze will function perfectly well with three, four or even more losers. But if the defender has exit cards which will need to be squeezed out the declarer must once again rectify his loser count by ducking down to two losers.

The basic triple squeeze, on the other hand, matures with two losers because a defender is busy in three suits. The associated three-suit strip-squeeze will thus take effect when declarer has three losers if the necessary compensation exists.

I would apologize for inflicting this chunk of theory on you but for the fact that a thorough understanding of the loser count requirements for different types of squeezes is vital.

♠ Q 7 4
♡ Q
◇ K Q 7 2   *Game all*
♣ A K 9 6 3

	West	North	East	South
			1 ◇	1 ♠

♠ J 10 9 6 5 3
♡ A J 10 5   —   4 ♠   all pass
◇ 6
♣ 10 4

West leads the nine of diamonds against your four spade contract and East plays the ace on dummy's queen. Unkindly, East switches to trumps, leading out the ace, king and another while his partner discards two small hearts. How do you plan the play?

There are only eight top tricks and to have any chance you must assume that the heart finesse is right. But that still leaves the tenth trick to find. It is a pity that you could not interchange your knave of hearts and dummy's queen, for then you could easily bring pressure to bear upon East. By ruffing a diamond, running the trumps and cashing dummy's top clubs you could subject East to a simple heart-diamond squeeze. But the blockage in hearts defeats that plan and it may seem that the only hope is that one of the defenders has both club honours. If West has the club honours a double finesse would bring home the contract, while if East has them he could be squeezed in hearts and clubs.

There is a better play, however, which will allow you to make your contract when the club honours are divided and also when East has them both. After winning the third round of trumps in dummy you should lead the queen of hearts for a finesse. East will play low to this trick, of course, and you will continue by cashing the ace of clubs, taking care to unblock the ten from your hand. The king of diamonds should be played for a heart discard and you should then ruff a diamond. Now the play of the last two trumps will create dire trouble for East in the following ending.

♠ —
♡ —
◇ 7
♣ K 9 6

♠ 10
♡ A J
◇ —
♣ 4

On the last spade you throw the six of clubs from dummy and East feels the pinch. Forced to keep two hearts and a diamond, he will have to throw his club honour, thereby exposing his partner to a simple finesse. This is the variant of the one-loser triple squeeze known as the guard squeeze, in which one defender has the too-onerous task of protecting two suits and guarding his partner against a finesse in a third.

Two points of technique are worth emphasizing. First, the guard menace must not be accompanied by more than one winner at the time the squeeze card is led. If you had not cashed the ace of clubs earlier the guard squeeze would not work, for East would have an idle card to throw on the last trump. Secondly, when applying pressure to the opponent on the right of the squeeze card, the menace in the same hand as the squeeze card must be accompanied by at least one winner. In the diagram above if the ace of hearts is cashed before the last spade the squeeze fails because dummy is squeezed ahead of East.

Another point of interest is that the squeeze will still succeed even in the unlikely event of West also controlling the fourth round of diamonds. The form is exactly the same, but we now call it a double guard squeeze since both opponents are squeezed. East is the first to feel the pressure when the last trump is played. If he keeps two hearts and the club honour and counts on his partner to protect diamonds he will be disappointed, for the lead of the ace of hearts will now inflict a simple club-diamond squeeze on West.

♠ A K Q J 9 7 3 2
♡ K
♢ 9 4
♣ 10 2

Love all

South	North
1 ♡	2 ♠
2 NT	4 ♠
6 NT	—

♠ 6 5
♡ A Q 7 4
♢ K Q J
♣ A J 6 3

West leads the nine of clubs against your six no trump contract and East puts on the queen. How do you plan the play?

You thought it would be better to have the lead coming up to your hand, but you see sadly that six spades would be a cinch on any lead. How are you going to make six no trumps on this diabolical club lead? Are you thinking of ducking in the hope that East will not find the diamond switch? If so you should think again. East will certainly cash the ace of diamonds if he has it, and if he hasn't your slam is unbeatable.

On the run of the spades neither defender will be able to keep three hearts, his own winner, *and* a card in his partner's suit. You could go wrong in the ending, of course, but as long as you keep count of the hearts and watch the discards closely you should have a good chance of getting it right. The last four cards in your hand will be the ace, queen and seven of hearts and the king of diamonds. If both defenders abandon hearts you can simply overtake dummy's king. Otherwise you will play the seven on dummy's king and exit towards whichever opponent you think has two hearts left.

A double squeeze in which a trick is given up after the squeeze is not at all common. When it does occur there is almost always some blocked entry position as in the heart suit in this hand. This is not really a two-loser squeeze, of course. You had twelve winners from the start; only the blockage made it difficult to cash them.

♠ A K 9 6 4
♡ 3   *Game all*
◇ K Q 8 6
♣ A K 7

West	North	East	South
		1 ♡	—
—	2 ♡	—	3 ♣
—	3 ♠	—	3 NT
—	4 ♣	—	4 ♡
—	6 ♣	all pass	

♠ 2
♡ A Q 7
◇ 7 5 4 2
♣ Q J 10 6 3

Against your six club contract West leads the two of hearts, East plays the king and you win with the ace. How should you continue?

You can count five club tricks, two spades, two hearts and a heart ruff, but only one diamond since the ace is sure to be with East. That is a total of eleven tricks. The twelfth will have to come from spades, which means the suit will need to break 4–3. Even then there could be difficulty in getting into dummy to cash that last spade. By the time you have ruffed a heart, ruffed two spades and drawn trumps you will have no trumps left. If you cash the queen of hearts at this stage the suit will be wide open when you let East in with the ace of diamonds, but if you don't cash the heart queen you will be a trick short.

Would it perhaps be possible to overcome this entry trouble by leading a diamond at the second trick? That will certainly work all right if East wins and switches, but a good player in the East seat will surely not do that. He will duck the first round of diamonds, or win and return the suit, either of which actions will defeat your slam by denying you the later entry you need to cash the last spade.

What else is there to play for? There is a chance that East's ace of diamonds is a singleton, of course, but it is a rather slender chance. The best plan is to play East for a 3–5–3–2 distribution and reconsider the line of play you thought of originally.

First you should play the ace and king of clubs to test the position, for if the trumps are 4–1 you will have to rely on East having the singleton ace of diamonds after all. If the trumps behave decently, however, you can continue with the ace and king of spades, a spade ruff in hand, a heart ruff on the table and a further spade ruff, reducing the position to the following:

♠ 9
♡ —
♢ K Q 8 6
♣ —

♠ —
♡ Q
♢ 7 5 4
♣ Q

Now your queen of clubs will draw the last trump while the six of diamonds goes from dummy, and East will feel the pinch in an unfamiliar way. He has already thrown a heart on the fourth spade and if he lets another one go the queen of hearts will extract his last one, making it perfectly safe for you to lead a diamond. If East chooses to part with a diamond, on the other hand, you can well afford not to cash the queen of hearts for you will now make an extra diamond trick.

The neat little strip-squeeze enables you to trim East's heart suit down to size, dummy's extra length in diamonds compensating for the fact that the entry position is irregular. It is not too easy to foresee the possibilities of this ending at the beginning of the hand.

♠ A K Q 6 3
♡ 8 7
◇ A K Q 10 4   *Game all*
♣ J   *North   South*
                                2 ♠   3 ♣
♠ 8 5 2   3 ◇   6 NT
♡ A K 5
◇ 7 5 3
♣ K Q 10 9

West leads the knave of spades against your six no trump contract. You put on the queen from dummy and East makes you blink by discarding the three of hearts. You test the diamonds by leading out the ace and king and West discards the two of clubs on the second round. How should you continue?

Once you knock out the ace of clubs you will have eleven top tricks. The twelfth will have to come from a squeeze. You have a spade menace against West and a diamond menace against East and an adequate double menace in the five of hearts. The position is known as an inverted double squeeze, and it will function automatically because the double menace is accompanied by two winners.

However, you have to think about what the opponents will do to you when you let them in with the ace of clubs. If they are kind enough to return a club your double automatic squeeze will remain intact. You will simply discard one card from each of dummy's suits on your clubs, whereupon the play of your spade and diamond winners in either order will squeeze each defender in turn out of his heart guard. Nor will it trouble you if West wins the ace of clubs and returns a spade. That will permit you to win in dummy, play off the queen of diamonds and come to hand with a heart to run the clubs for a positional double squeeze.

The killing defence is a heart return. This will defeat you by converting the automatic squeeze to a positional one which will fail because the queen of diamonds has not been played off. The effect of the heart return is to remove an idle card from dummy, thus making it impossible for you to run the clubs without squeezing dummy first. You could recover if you could somehow manage to cash the queen of diamonds and get back to hand without destroying your heart entry, but that is just not possible.

East in particular is certain to return a heart if he gets in with the ace of clubs, and it logically follows that you are not going to make this slam when East has the club ace. That being so, you may as well assume the club ace to be with West, for that will simplify the problem. The way to make sure of twelve tricks whenever West has the club ace is to cash the queen of diamonds before leading clubs.

Now a heart return from West will have no terrors for you. By running the clubs you reach the position shown below.

♠ A K 6
♡ 8
♢ 10
♣ —

♠ 8 5
♡ A 5
♢ —
♣ 9

There can be no ambiguity since you know West's precise spade holding. When you lead the last club West must, in order to retain his spade guard, come down to a single heart. Dummy's six of spades, having done its job, can now be discarded, and you switch the pressure to East by playing off the two top spades. Holding the knave of diamonds and two hearts, East may do whatever gives him the most pleasure.

♠ K 7 3
♡ Q 9 4
♢ Q 9 8   *North-South game*
♣ A 10 3 2

West	North	East	South
—	—	—	1 ♠

♠ A Q 10 6 5 4
♡ A 2   —   2 NT   —   4 ♠
♢ J 6 5 3   all pass
♣ Q

West leads the eight of hearts against your four spade contract.
You put in the nine from dummy, East plays the ten and you win
with the ace. When you cash the ace of spades West startles you
by discarding the six of clubs. There is a danger that East may get
a diamond ruff if trumps are not drawn straight away, so you
continue with three more rounds, finessing against East's knave
while West discards the five and four of clubs and the five of
hearts. What do you throw from dummy on the fourth spade?

It is always difficult to have to make a crucial discard at an
early stage, and it is far from obvious that the only card you can
spare from dummy is a heart. But a careful study of the available
evidence can point to no other conclusion. It seems a reasonably
safe inference that East started with nine cards in the major suits
and West with length in the minors, probably including six clubs to
judge from his discards. There are indications from both the bidding
and the play that the top diamond honours are likely to be divided.
Your best chance, therefore, will be to lead a small diamond at
the next trick with the intention of finessing dummy's eight.

If West plays high on this trick and returns a heart it will make
no difference whether you have one or two hearts left in dummy.
And if West plays low and the eight of diamonds draws the ace or
king from East, you must be prepared for the possibility of a club
return knocking out dummy's ace. Then, unless you are willing to
bank on a 3–3 diamond break, you will have to return to your
hand by ruffing a club in order to lead another diamond towards
dummy. If West has A 10 x or K 10 x left in diamonds he will play
high on the second round so as to block the suit, and now the
reason for keeping that extra club in dummy becomes apparent.

With only one club remaining in his hand, West will be unable to lead the suit without presenting you with the contract. Instead he will have to exit with a heart to his partner's king, and East will perforce return a heart in the following ending.

When you ruff East's heart return West will be caught in a jettison squeeze. Throwing the master club makes dummy's cards good, while a diamond discard permits you to jettison the blocking queen from dummy.

Variations in the defence can lead to slightly different endings. If West wins the first diamond and attacks hearts and East continues with hearts when he gets in, for instance, the position will be as follows.

The jettison squeeze is still there as long as West has both the king and the knave of clubs.

♠ K 8
♡ J 10 8 7
♢ A 10 3   *Love all*
♣ A Q 6 5

	West	*North*	*East*	*South*
			1 ♡	4 ♠
♠ Q J 10 9 7 5 3 2	—	6 ♠	all pass	
♡ —				
♢ K J 7				
♣ 4 2				

West leads the two of hearts against your spade slam, East plays the queen on dummy's seven and you ruff. On your trump lead West plays the four, dummy the king and East the ace. East now returns the four of diamonds. How do you play?

This return takes care of one of your losers nicely. It looks as though East has been end-played at trick two. You will not need the club finesse for your contract, but you will require a diamond entry to dummy later, so you should play your knave on this trick. Whether or not the knave is covered the next trick should be won by dummy's eight of trumps and the knave of hearts led to force a cover from East. After ruffing this trick you run three more trumps, discarding clubs from dummy, and reach this position.

♠ —
♡ 10 8
♢ A 10
♣ A

♠ 9
♡ —
♢ K 7
♣ 4 2

Two rounds of diamonds ending in dummy will now inflict a double ruffing squeeze on the defenders. Neither opponent can come down to a single heart without allowing you to set up a heart trick by ruffing, and if they both discard clubs your club four will take the last trick.

PRESSURE PLAY

East should, of course, have given you a chance to go wrong by playing the ace or king of hearts on the first trick.

♠ A 10 4
♡ K 3
◇ A J 9 2
♣ Q 8 7 4

North-South game

♠ 7
♡ A Q J 9 8 7 5 2
◇ K 8 3
♣ 9

South	North
4 ♡	4 NT
6 ♡	—

West leads the king of clubs against your six heart contract and East plays the knave. West switches to the queen of spades which you win with the ace, East dropping the nine. How do you plan the play?

If the diamond finesse is right you need not take it, for a club-diamond squeeze will serve just as well and give you an extra chance when East has the doubleton queen of diamonds.

But the best way to play this hand is as a double guard squeeze, which will succeed if West has either the queen or the ten of diamonds or both. Some careful unblocking in dummy will be needed. On the sixth and seventh hearts you must throw the nine and knave of diamonds, leaving the following position.

♠ 10
♡ —
◇ A 2
♣ Q

♠ —
♡ 5
◇ K 8 3
♣ —

At this stage West will have the knave of spades, the ace of clubs and two diamonds left, and the lead of the last heart will turn the screw. A spade discard exposes his partner to a spade-

167

diamond squeeze, so West will come down to a singleton diamond. Now a diamond to the ace drops his honour card, leaving a finessing position against East.

♠ K 9 4
♡ K 6
♢ A 5 3   *North-South game*
♣ Q J 8 6 2

West	North	East	South
		1 NT*	2 ♠

♠ A Q J 8 2
♡ J 7 4 3   —   4 ♠   all pass
♢ K J
♣ 10 4   * *12–14 points*

West leads the five of clubs against your four spade contract. East wins with the king and cashes the ace of clubs on which West plays the three. East continues with the nine of clubs which you ruff with the knave of spades while West discards the two of hearts. Both defenders follow with small cards when you play the ace of trumps. How should you continue?

To have any chance of making this contract you must assume that East has the queen of diamonds. Even so, there is no simple way of making the hand because of the block in communications. The problem is how to cross the table to take the diamond finesse and then return to dummy to enjoy the third diamond trick. But if you are toying with the idea of finessing the nine of spades on the second round you should forget it. This is not the proper occasion for such a hair-raising risk. On the assumption—a perfectly reasonable one—that the trumps will break evenly and that the diamond queen is with East, your contract is unbeatable.

On his opening bid East is marked with the ace of hearts, and if he has the diamond queen he cannot have the heart queen as well for that would give him a total of fifteen points. So the queen of hearts will be with West, and this is therefore one of the rare occasions on which you can squeeze both opponents in the same two suits.

168

You should continue by playing the queen of trumps and then a third round to dummy's king. Dummy's club winners should be cashed next while you discard two hearts from your hand. Then the finesse of the knave of diamonds will produce the following position.

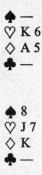

♠ —
♡ K 6
♢ A 5
♣ —

♠ 8
♡ J 7
♢ K
♣ —

On the lead of the eight of spades you can throw the six of hearts from dummy and both opponents will be under high pressure. If either defender bares his heart honour you will cash your king of diamonds and exit with a heart, while if they both throw diamonds you can overtake your king of diamonds with dummy's ace.

At first glance it appears that there might be some ambiguity in the situation—that you could be uncertain as to what exactly has happened after both defenders have played to the tenth trick. But this is not so. You will be perfectly safe as long as you keep track of the number of diamonds outstanding. After the tenth trick, if there are three diamonds left in the opponents' hands, it will always be safe to play off the diamond king and then exit with a heart. Should the defenders keep only two diamonds, the lead of the diamond king will provide you with the final piece of evidence. If West shows out you will play low in dummy and throw East in with the heart. But if West follows to the king of diamonds it is safe to overtake with dummy's ace. Either the remaining diamond will drop or your knave of hearts will take the last trick.

♠ J 6 4
♡ J 9 7 4 3   *Game all*
◇ A
♣ A K 8 3   *South*   *North*
                               1 ♡   3 ♣
                               3 ◇   3 ♡
♠ A K   3 ♠   4 ♣
♡ K Q 10 8   4 ♡   5 ◇
◇ 10 9 7 6 2   6 ♡   —
♣ J 5

West leads the two of trumps against your six heart contract. East takes the ace and returns the suit and West discards a small spade. How do you plan the play?

But for the trump lead a cross-ruff would probably have got you home, but now it looks as though you will need to find one opponent with K Q J bare in diamonds. Hopefully you lead a diamond to the ace, but both defenders play small cards.

The trouble is that even if the diamonds break 4–3 you have not enough entries in hand to ruff out the suit and cash the last diamond without allowing East to make his outstanding trump. But there is still a slight chance and you should continue with a spade to your king, a diamond ruff, a spade to the ace and another diamond ruff. The ace and king of clubs are followed by a club ruff, leaving the following position.

♠ J
♡ J
◇ —
♣ 8

♠ —
♡ K
◇ 10 9
♣ —

If East began with something like ♠ Q x x, ♡ A x x, ◇ Q x x, ♣ 10 x x x, he will come under pressure when you ruff the fourth diamond in dummy. It is an unusual type of trump squeeze wherein a defender is squeezed in three singletons, one of them a trump.

170

♠ 10 7 6
♡ K J 9 8 7 5 3
◇ 6
♣ K 4

Game all

West	North	East	South
1 ◇	3 ♡	—	6 NT
all pass			

♠ K J
♡ A 10 2
◇ A K 10
♣ A 9 7 5 2

West leads the queen of diamonds against your six no trump contract and you win with the ace. Both opponents follow with small cards to the lead of the ace of hearts. How should you continue?

You have eleven top tricks and a finesse against the spade queen could provide the twelfth, but on the bidding it is highly likely that West has both the ace and queen of spades. What are the squeeze prospects then? Although you have two losers and no way of rectifying the count this need not worry you unduly. West is sure to feel the pinch if you run the hearts down to this ending.

♠ 10 7 6
♡ 5
◇ —
♣ K 4

♠ K
♡
◇ K 10
♣ A 9 7

It is not necessary for West to have all the club honours. If he has any two of them the guard squeeze will cripple him when you lead dummy's last heart and discard your king of spades. The extension to the spade menace and the re-entry card in dummy allow the guard squeeze to operate smoothly with two losers, but it is worth noting that the squeeze would fail if you had not kept a diamond winner in hand.

♠ K Q J 10 9 3
♡ A 4 2
◇ 7 5
♣ Q 8

Love all

	South	West	North	East
	1 ◇	1 ♡	2 ♠	—
	3 ♣	—	3 ♠	—
	6 NT	all pass		

♠ 2
♡ K 9 5
◇ A K Q 9 3
♣ A 10 6 2

West leads the queen of hearts against your six no trump contract. You win in hand with the king and play on spades, and West wins the second round and continues with the knave of hearts. How do you plan the play?

There will be no problem if the diamonds break evenly of course. If East has long diamonds and the king of clubs you will have, in theory, a simple squeeze. In practice it may be very hard for you to read the position, and in any case the king of clubs is more likely to be with West. If West has long diamonds and the king of clubs there can be no simple squeeze, since you have been unable to employ the Vienna Coup by playing off the ace of clubs before running the spades.

Nevertheless there is still a way of achieving a sort of Vienna Coup even though it means deliberately increasing your loser count to two. On dummy's spades you should discard your heart and all your clubs, keeping the diamond suit intact. The point is that the value of the ace of clubs in this hand is illusory. If the diamonds are breaking you don't need it anyway, while if the diamonds split badly the discard of the club ace represents your only chance of making the contract. If West started with ♠ A x, ♡ Q J 10 x x, ◇ 10 x x x, ♣ K x he will be subjected to a triple squeeze, the standard form of which, as you know, matures with two losers in hand. What is more, thanks to the extended menace in diamonds, the squeeze is sure to repeat, thereby gaining the two tricks you need for your contract.

♠ J 4
♡ A Q
◇ A J 3
♣ A K Q J 7 2   *Game all*

West	North	East	South
—	2 ♣	2 ♠	2 NT
—	4 NT	—	6 NT
all pass			

♠ A 7 3 2
♡ J 10 5
◇ K 8 4
♣ 9 8 6

West leads the eight of spades against your six no trump contract, you play low from dummy and East puts in the nine. How do you plan the play?

For his hazardous spade bid East should have the heart king and the diamond queen. Since you have ten top tricks and three losers your first thought is to duck in order to rectify the count for a triple squeeze against East. But closer inspection shows that the triple squeeze will gain only one trick. It cannot repeat provided that East gives up his diamond guard, for after three rounds of diamonds there will be no further means of communication between your hand and dummy's. There is no need to despair, though. The three-suit strip-squeeze, which functions with three losers, will come to your aid. You should win the first trick and run the clubs to reach this position.

♠ J
♡ A Q
◇ A J 3
♣ 2

♠ 7 3 2
♡ J
◇ K 8
♣ —

On the last club East must unguard one of the red suits in order to retain two spades. The play of the suit he unguarded will then squeeze him again. The basic reason why the strip-squeeze works where the standard squeeze fails is that you have retained the option of leading spades from dummy.

♠ 6
♡ K 9 3
◇ A 8 7 4   *North-South game*
♣ Q J 8 6 2

	West	North	East	South
	3 ♠	—	—	3 NT
	—	4 NT	—	6 NT
	all pass			

♠ A K Q
♡ A 8 6 5 2
◇ K Q 3
♣ K 10

West leads the ten of hearts against your six no trump contract. You win in hand and play the king of clubs, and East takes the ace and returns the queen of hearts to dummy's king. West follows to this trick, but when you play a club to your ten he discards a spade. How should you continue?

On the bidding East is quite likely to have length in diamonds as well. Unfortunately there is no simple squeeze on this hand. There are no entries for a heart-club squeeze, a heart-diamond squeeze will fail because you cannot cash dummy's club winners without destroying the diamond entry, and in a diamond-club squeeze dummy will feel the pressure before East.

You can, however, cash two top spades without damaging dummy (the nine of hearts can be thrown), and in doing so you may find that you have squeezed East after all. Because you have only one loser, East, who has the task of guarding three suits, is squeezed on the play of your *second* last winner in the fourth suit, at a time when dummy has still an idle card to play.

This one-loser triple squeeze is of small interest in itself, because it is only when there is a blocked position as in the clubs above that the hand will not reduce to a simpler squeeze. In compound squeeze play, however, where one opponent is squeezed in three suits and the other in two, the position cannot be reduced because of the need to keep menaces against both defenders. The importance of the one-loser triple squeeze is that it forms the backbone of all compound squeeze play.

174

♠ 6
♡ A K 9 6 4
♦ A K 8 5 3   *North-South game*
♣ 5 4

	South	*West*	*North*	*East*
♠ K Q J 10	1 ♣	1 ♠	3 ♡	—
♡ 10 5	4 ♣	—	4 ♦	—
♦ J 6	6 NT	all pass		
♣ A K Q J 6				

Against your favourite contract West leads the ace of spades, East follows with the seven, and West switches to the two of diamonds. How should you play?

Five club tricks will make you happy, so assume clubs break badly. West is unlikely to hold five clubs and if he does there is probably no squeeze. If East has length in clubs, on the other hand, a squeeze is sure to be present. The only problem is in deciding which squeeze to go for. There are intriguing double guard squeeze possibilities using either diamonds or hearts as the guard menace, but a compound squeeze will bring home the slam no matter where the red suit honours lie.

You should win the ace of diamonds, come to hand with a club, and rattle off three spades, discarding two hearts and a diamond (or, if you feel strongly about it, two diamonds and a heart) from dummy. If East has club length he will be forced to give up protection in one of the red suits. As this is a one-loser triple squeeze East will, in fact, be squeezed twice by your second last and your last spades, and this should make it fairly clear which suit he has abandoned. You then cash the top cards in that suit to squeeze East out of his guard in the other red suit, whereupon the run of the clubs will inflict a red suit squeeze on West.

Note that you cannot afford to test the clubs before finishing the spades. You can find out about the bad club break only by taking out your last entry, and it is then too late to effect the squeeze.

♠ A 5
♡ A 9 7 6 4
◇ 6 5 3   *Game all*
♣ A 8 6

	South	North
	2 ♠	4 NT
	7 ♠	—

♠ K Q J 10 8 6 3
♡ K
◇ A K 2
♣ J 5

West leads the queen of hearts against your grand slam, and East follows with the two. How should you plan the play?

With twelve top tricks you will have to look to a squeeze for the thirteenth. It looks as though West is the only defender with a heart stopper, in which case the slam can certainly be made by compound squeeze play.

The correct sequence is to win the second trump in dummy, cash the ace of hearts discarding a club from your hand, then ruff a heart before running the spades. The one-loser triple squeeze will pinch West on the lead of your second last trump and he will have to unguard one of the minor suits.

♠ —
♡ 9
◇ 6 5
♣ A 8

♠ 6
♡ —
◇ A K 2
♣ J

The last spade starts the non-simultaneous double squeeze. A diamond is thrown from dummy and East is the first to succumb, being forced to unguard the minor suit his partner is protecting. Now your play varies according to which suits the opponents have kept. If West has retained diamonds and East clubs, the play of the ace of clubs gives the *coup de grace* to West. Otherwise, the play of the ace and king of diamonds will finish him.

In compound squeeze play the main difficulty is to determine what has happened when you reach the crossroads. Often your decision has to be made before the play of the final squeeze card, and then it can be really tough. In this case, however, you can run the whole trump suit before making up your mind. Since West has to make two discards after the squeeze it should not be too hard to determine which suit he has given up.

Note that it would be a mistake not to cash the ace of hearts before running the trumps, for correct defence by West would then defeat you. This is because the opponent who is triple squeezed can choose, by giving up one suit or the other, the type of double squeeze available to you in the end game. You must therefore try to plan the early play so as to be able to cope with any eventuality. Suppose you had left the ace of hearts in dummy and reduced to this position.

```
        ♠ —
        ♡ A 9
        ◇ 6 5
        ♣ A 8


        ♠ 6
        ♡ —
        ◇ A K 2
        ♣ J 5
```

If West has come down to one club you are all right, for the inverted double automatic squeeze will function equally well with the ace of hearts still in dummy. But if West has given up his diamond guard you can wave good-bye to the grand slam, for the only squeeze left to you is a positional one. With clubs as the double menace you cannot squeeze East without first playing off the ace of hearts, but you are unable to do that without destroying the entry to the double menace.

It is also worth noting that an initial club or diamond lead would have rendered your squeeze stillborn.

♠ K 9 3
♡ K J 7   *Game all*
◇ A K 8
♣ A K 9 5   North   South
                 2 NT   3 ♡
♠ A 5 4   4 ♣   4 ♠
♡ A Q 10 8 6 4   5 ◇   6 ♣
◇ 5 3 2   6 ◇   7 ♡
♣ 4

Another grand slam and a further exercise in compound squeeze technique. How should you play after West's lead of the queen of clubs?

Again, on the reasonable assumption that only West can guard the clubs, you can squeeze out the thirteenth trick for sure if you read the discards correctly. The proper play is to win the third round of trumps in dummy, ruff the small club and lead your second last trump.

♠ K 9 3
♡ —
◇ A K 8
♣ K 9

♠ A 5 4
♡ Q 10
◇ 5 3 2
♣ —

This is one of the tricky situations where you have to judge which suit West has given up before leading your final squeeze card. After West discards on the queen of hearts, if you think he has abandoned diamonds, you should discard the diamond eight from dummy. Then cash the two top diamonds and the king of clubs, discarding a spade from hand, and return to the ace of spades to lead the last heart and inflict the double positional squeeze.

178

PRESSURE PLAY

If West gives up his spade guard you must discard a spade from dummy on the second last heart. Then, after a spade to the king, a diamond discard on the king of clubs and a spade back to the ace, the last trump gives them the business as before.

It is a little puzzling to see that, while in the last hand it would have been wrong to leave an entry-less winner in dummy, in this case it would be incorrect to cash the club king at an earlier stage. The reason is that all the cards in your hand are busy: you cannot know what you want to discard on the king of clubs until after the one-loser triple squeeze has done its work on West.

Suppose you discarded a diamond on the king of clubs before effecting the squeeze. West could now defeat you by giving up diamonds. Similarly, if you threw a spade on the king of clubs West would beat you by giving up his spade guard.

In this squeeze it can do no harm to leave the king of clubs in dummy because your entry position is such that you will always be able to cash the club king later without prejudicing any double squeeze that may eventuate.

CHAPTER 9

Match Point

No book on the play of the hand at bridge would be complete without a chapter on match-point pairs. This form of the game is rather different from rubber or team-of-four bridge and has problems all of its own. The exigencies of match-point scoring are such that you have to modify your tactics, sometimes making plays that would be wildly unsound at any other form of bridge.

Players new to the pairs game find it hard to understand that the making of the contract has not the same overriding importance as in rubber bridge. The main objective is to obtain a bigger plus score, or a smaller minus score, than the other pairs who are playing the same cards as you.

This causes some distortion of the bidding, of course, since players tend to favour no trumps and avoid minor suit contracts, particularly at the game level. Part-score bidding is fiercely competitive and close doubles are often made. But here we are concerned only with the way in which the match-point scoring affects the declarer's play.

MATCH POINT

The advice to take a little time for thinking before playing to the first trick applies with even greater force to match-point pairs. For here it is not just a matter of deciding on the best or the safest way of playing the hand: you have other things to think about. First you must evaluate your contract in the light of what may happen, or may have happened, at the other tables. Only thus can you decide correctly on the number of tricks you will need to earn a good match-point score. Possibly it will suffice to make your contract, perhaps you will need over-tricks, or it could be that one down will give you a top score. The target of tricks you have to set yourself will not always coincide with the number of tricks needed for the contract.

When your contract is a normal one and you judge that most of the other pairs will be in it, all you need do is play to take as many tricks as you can. But if good judgement has landed you in a distributional game call which you think few other pairs will reach you may decide to consolidate your advantage by playing as safely as possible. On occasion you may slip up in the bidding and find yourself in a poor contract. Then your only chance of snatching a few match points will be to dream up some adverse distribution that will cause the correct contract to fail and play for that distribution to exist. This often applies when you have underbid and stopped short of a game contract that most players will be in. You must assume that the game will fail and make sure of your own plus score. The opposite situation arises when you have overbid. Then you must go all out for your contract, taking whatever risks are needed, since you will get a very poor score if you go down.

The opening lead often has a profound influence on your tactical match-point decisions. A lead that presents you with a trick you could not otherwise have made will no doubt cause you to play safely down the middle, taking no chance of giving the trick back to the opponents. But when you receive a lead that places you at a disadvantage compared with other declarers, you must take risks in an effort to draw level again.

181

♠ 10 4
♡ Q 10 6
◇ 7 6
♣ A 8 7 5 4 2

Love all

South	North
1 ♡	2 ♡
—	

♠ J 7 5 2
♡ K J 9 3
◇ A K 4
♣ K 3

Against your two heart contract West leads the two of trumps to his partner's ace. East returns the five of hearts, West follows with the four and you win with dummy's ten. How should you continue?

Here you have a typical match-point decision to make. You can be fairly sure of eight tricks by ruffing a diamond in dummy, but will that be enough to earn you a good score? It is possible that ten tricks can be made by ruffing the third round of clubs with your king and re-entering dummy in trumps.

It is by no means certain that everyone will play this hand in hearts, however. To do a proper job of evaluation you must also consider the number of tricks that will be available in the other likely contracts. Some players will open with one no trump on your hand, and they could be left to play there. Other pairs could well play in two or three clubs. You can see that the limit is likely to be seven tricks in no trumps, and nine in clubs if the suit breaks 3–2.

Thus if you score 110 for making eight tricks in hearts you will beat any pair who plays in no trumps, and at worst tie with those who play in clubs. In other words, just making your contract should give you a better than average score. Don't be greedy, then. Be satisfied with eight tricks.

Only if you met this hand late in a tournament when you knew you needed a few top scores to bring you into the prize list would you be justified in gambling on a 3–3 heart break and a 3–2 club break and trying for ten tricks.

MATCH POINT

♠ K Q 9 8 3
♡ Q
♢ Q 5 4
♣ A J 10 5

North-South game

♠ 10
♡ A J 5
♢ A J 10 7 6 2
♣ K 6 3

South	North
1 ♢	1 ♠
2 ♢	3 ♣
3 NT	—

To your surprise, West leads the knave of spades against your three no trump contract. East covers dummy's queen with the ace and returns the four of hearts. How do you plan the play?

Perhaps the spade lead was not as favourable as it first appeared to be. Presumably the knave was singleton or doubleton so you will have gained nothing in the spade suit, while this heart return is awkward. Seeing the bare queen in dummy, East would not have led from the king.

You can always make sure of ten tricks, eleven for that matter if the diamond finesse is right. But will that be good enough? Other declarers will very likely get a heart lead away from the king, or even a club from the queen. They will be in a position to take the diamond finesse before knocking out the ace of spades, and they will make a trick more than you whether the diamond king is right or wrong. The opening lead has thus placed you at a disadvantage compared with the other declarers, and you must take serious risks, even to the extent of jeopardizing your contract, in order to recover.

Your proper play is the ace of hearts, followed by a club to the ace and the three winning spades, discarding the two remaining hearts and a club from your hand. Now hold your breath and take the diamond finesse. If it loses you will get a complete bottom instead of a near-bottom, but if it wins you will do as well as any other declarer in three no trumps.

```
♠ J 10 4
♡ K 2
♢ 9 7 6                    Game all
♣ A Q 8 6 5
                    South    North
                     1 ♠      2 ♣
♠ K Q 9 8 3          2 NT     3 ♠
♡ Q J 6              4 ♠      —
♢ A K 8
♣ 7 2
```

West leads the ace and another trump against your four spade contract and East follows both times. You win in hand and lead the six of hearts to dummy's king, but East takes the ace and produces the last trump. How do you plan the play?

The hand is developing unfavourably for you. But for the repeated trump leads you would have been able to discard one of dummy's diamonds on an established heart and eventually to ruff a diamond in dummy. Of course you will still be able to make ten tricks if the club finesse is right, but that will do you no good for 620 will be a very poor score. With the club finesse working, all the South players who do not receive a trump lead against four spades will make eleven tricks and score 650. And anyone playing in three no trumps will probably score 630 for ten tricks.

To get a reasonable score on this hand you must assume that the club finesse is wrong, in which case nobody will make more than ten tricks at spades and nine at no trumps. If you can make your contract you will beat the no trumpers and tie with the others playing in spades. The only legitimate chance is that East has the doubleton king of clubs, but you should be able to augment this 8 per cent chance considerably by playing a small club from the table at the fifth trick. If East holds the king but not the knave of clubs he will have a difficult guess whether to play his king or not.

♠ 10 7
♡ K Q 6 4
◇ 10 6 5
♣ K 9 4 2   *East-West game*

♠ A 8 3   *South*   *West*   *North*   *East*
♡ A J 8 3   1 NT   all pass
◇ J 7 4
♣ Q J 6

West leads the five of spades against your one no trump contract. East plays the king and you win the trick with the ace. How should you continue?

It is not hard to see that you are in the wrong contract. Anyone playing in two hearts is likely to have little trouble in making eight tricks. It is one of the hazards of using the weak no trump that you are apt, on occasion, to miss 4–4 major suit fits at a low level.

You have no chance of beating the pairs who play in two hearts. But will there be many of them? The merits as well as the defects of the weak no trump are apparent on this deal. Your one no trump opening appears to have been effective in keeping the opponents out of the bidding. But anyone who opens with one heart is likely to hear a one spade overcall on his left, and it is probable that at most tables West will be the declarer in two spades. Counting your defensive tricks you see that you have a maximum of five—one spade, two hearts and two clubs. East-West can therefore make eight or nine tricks in spades for a score of 110 or 140.

This leads inevitably to the conclusion that you should not try to steal a club trick on this hand, since that would risk going three down for a very bad score. You should simply take your five tricks secure in the knowledge that minus 100 should bring you in quite a number of match points.

♠ K 7 4 3
♡ 9 8 6
◇ 6 4   *East-West game*
♣ 10 8 7 2

South	West	North	East
1 ♠	—	2 ♠	Double

♠ A 8 6 5 2

4 ♣	5 ♡	5 ♠	—

♡ A
◇ K 9 7 5 3

—	Double	all pass	

♣ 6 3

Against your doubled contract of five spades West leads the four of hearts to East's queen. How do you plan the play?

Presumably your partner thought there was no defence against five hearts, but his action in pushing on to five spades without giving you the chance to voice an opinion was dubious. It is likely that most North-South pairs will choose to defend against five hearts. In such cases you must always assume your sacrifice to be worth while. You must base your play on the assumption that the opponents can make five hearts, in which case you can afford to go three down but not four.

On the bidding East is likely to be short in spades, but he will not be void, for then West would have an automatic trump lead. East's spade holding can just about be pin-pointed as the singleton knave or ten. So in five hearts West would have a spade and a trump to lose, and you must assume he would lose no diamond trick. If West has a singleton diamond it does not matter how you play, but if he has more than one diamond you must assume he has the ace. In that case it would be not only pointless but dangerous for you to cross to dummy in trumps in order to lead a diamond towards your king. That would allow West to play a second round of trumps, and he might be able to win the next diamond lead and draw a third round of trumps, which would give you a bottom score if diamonds break 4–2.

The correct play is a low diamond from hand at trick two.

MATCH POINT

♠ K J 4
♡ Q 6 5 3
◇ 10 7 6 4 2
♣ A

Game all

	South	*North*
	1 ♠	2 ◇
	2 NT	3 NT

♠ A 10 9 8 3
♡ A J
◇ J 5
♣ K Q 7 2

West leads the two of hearts against your three no trump contract. How should you plan the play?

Your partner's action in raising to three no trumps without showing his spade support was unorthodox, to say the least. It seems probable that most South players will be playing this hand in a contract of four spades, and you should take this into account in determining your best line of play. If the declarers in four spades succeed in catching the queen of trumps and find the heart finesse right for them they will probably make a trick more than you. After testing the hearts and ruffing a club in dummy it will be natural for them to play East for the queen of spades, so perhaps it would be a bright idea for you to bank on West having the queen and finesse the other way.

But there is another important factor that you should take into consideration—the opening lead. A lead from four to the king would be quite normal against no trumps, but less attractive against a four spade contract. It will be quite unnecessary for you to play differently from the four spade declarers if the opening lead has already presented you with the extra trick you need to beat them.

It is vital to find out whether or not the opening lead has given you a present, and the only certain way of doing this is by playing the queen of hearts from dummy on the first trick. If the queen holds you can relax and play the spades naturally, cashing dummy's king and then running the knave if East plays low.

Should East cover the heart queen with the king, on the other hand, the opening lead has given you nothing and you will have to outguess the four spade declarers as to the position of the spade queen. After winning the ace of hearts you should lead the ten of spades and run it.

♠ J 9 4 2
♡ A 6 4
◇ Q 3
♣ 8 7 6 3   *Love all*

♠ Q 5
♡ K J 8 7 2
◇ K 9 4
♣ A 10 4

South	West	North	East
1 NT	all pass		

West starts with the two of diamonds against your one no trump contract. You try the queen from dummy, but East wins with the ace and returns the five of diamonds. How should you plan the play?

Suppressing your five card major suit has landed you in a spot of trouble. All the strong no trump adherents, and even some of the weak no trumpers, will open one heart on your hand and will play in the more comfortable contract of two hearts. By playing to ruff a diamond in dummy they are likely to make eight tricks when the heart finesse is right.

You will be able to make seven tricks at no trumps by taking the same successful finesse, but that would bring you in precious little in the way of match points. You need luck on your side on this board, for your only chance to score well is to assume that West has the queen and one other heart. If the long shot comes off you will make your contract by playing for the drop while the pairs in the better contract of two hearts are going one down.

Bridge can at times be a very unfair game.

MATCH POINT

♠ J 10 9 4
♡ 10 8 7 4
♢ K 6 3
♣ 9 4

Game all

♠ —
♡ A Q 9 6 3 2
♢ A 7 2
♣ 10 7 6 5

South	West	North	East
1 ♡	—	2 ♡	Double
4 ♡	4 ♠	—	—
5 ♡	Double	all pass	

West leads the three of spades against your doubled five heart contract. East plays the king on dummy's nine and you ruff and lead a small club. East wins this trick with the knave and switches to the queen of diamonds which you take with the ace, West playing the four. A further club lead is won by East's king and the knave of diamonds is returned. West follows with the five and you win with dummy's king. How should you continue?

It is by no means certain that you made the right decision in going on over four spades, but you are booked for a poor score if you were wrong so you must assume that four spades can be made. In defence against that contract you would have a certain trump trick and two diamond tricks. To give you a chance of some match points one of the opponents (certainly East on the bidding) will need to be void in hearts. In that case it would be fatal to test the trumps. Your only chance of getting out for two down is to try to bring about some sort of trump end-play against West.

You should ruff a spade, ruff a club in dummy, ruff another spade and lead your last club. If West trumps in you can discard dummy's losing diamond, but if he is out of clubs West is more likely to discard a spade, in which case you will ruff in dummy and exit with the diamond. With A Q 9 in trumps left in your hand you are now assured of the two additional tricks you need to limit your loss to 500, which could be a useful score.

189

MATCH POINT

♠ J 10 9 6 4
♡ A 10
♢ Q 4
♣ A K J 3

East-West game

	South	North
	1 ♠	3 ♣
	3 ♢	4 ♠

♠ K Q 8 5 2
♡ J 4 3
♢ A 10 6 2
♣ 8

West leads the eight of hearts against your four spade contract. How should you plan the play?

At the most you will lose a spade, a heart and a diamond, so your contract is in no danger. The trouble is that 620 is likely to be very close to a bottom score for you. Not every South player will consider his hand to have the makings of an opening bid. At the majority of tables it is likely that North will be the declarer at four spades. And it is all too plain that any side suit lead would permit North to make eleven tricks without the slightest difficulty. Even if South does play the hand at some other tables he could get a diamond lead which would give him his eleventh trick, or a club which would permit him to try for the eleventh trick without risk.

When a combination of unfavourable events puts you at a disadvantage like this, the only thing to do is to live dangerously. You must do what you would never dream of doing at any other form of bridge—risk your contract in an effort to catch up with the other declarers. The proper course is to win the heart lead with the ace, come to hand with the ace of diamonds, and lead your club for a finesse of the knave. If the finesse loses you will go down in your contract and score a cold bottom instead of a near bottom, but if the knave of clubs wins you will have a good chance of getting both your losing hearts away, which will give you eleven tricks and an average score on the hand.

190

MATCH POINT

```
♠ J 10 3
♡ A 7 2
♢ 7 6 4 2                East-West game
♣ K 10 6
                    West    North    East    South
♠ 7                          —        —      3 ◇
♡ Q 4               Double  5 ◇     Double  all pass
♢ A Q J 9 5 3
♣ 7 5 4 2
```

West leads the knave of hearts against your doubled contract of five diamonds. Since he is not likely to have led away from a king on this bidding and you don't want to run into club ruffs, you put on dummy's ace and lead a diamond. East plays the eight, you finesse the knave, and West discards the three of clubs. How should you continue?

Your partner's tactics in raising to the limit may pay off, since East-West clearly have a game in spades. You can therefore afford to go three down and still get a useful score.

East is known to have the king of diamonds, presumably he has the king of hearts, and he probably has the spade king as well seeing that West did not lead the suit. Then the club ace will certainly be with West, and dummy's king could provide the entry for a second trump finesse. You might escape for 300.

However, it is unlikely to make much difference to your matchpoint score whether you lose 300 or 500. The one thing you must at all costs avoid is a loss of 700. That could come about if you lead a club now and East turns out to have a singleton in the suit. West would win with the ace and lead the queen, East would ruff dummy's king and put his partner back in with a spade to cash the club knave. A fourth round of clubs would now permit East to over-ruff dummy.

The scissors coup can come to the rescue here. By leading your spade at trick three you will be sure of holding your loss to 500 while retaining the chance of losing only 300.

191

♠ 8 6 5 3
♡ A 9 3
◊ K   *Game all*
♣ K J 8 7 5

                       South   *North*
                       1 ♠   3 ♠

♠ A K 9 4 2
♡ 4   4 ♠   —
◊ A Q 6 4 2
♣ 6 3

West leads the queen of hearts against your four spade contract. You put on dummy's ace and East plays the eight. How should you continue?

Barring a vile trump break your contract should be safe enough, so this is primarily a matter of making overtricks. Some players would come to hand with the ace of trumps and put West immediately to the test by the lead of a club. It is true that this might induce a nervous West to go up with the ace if he has it, although not knowing about your diamond length, he has no logical reason for doing so.

There is quite a good chance of a 2–2 trump break, however, in which case there will be a better way of playing on West's nerves. At trick two you should cash the king of diamonds, lead a trump to the ace, then ruff a small diamond in dummy. After a second round of trumps you can lead out your diamonds from the top, discarding dummy's remaining hearts. If you get the normal 4–3 break and East follows to four rounds, you should cash the fifth diamond as well, making sure that West knows you had five spades and five diamonds originally. Now when you lead a club it is hardly possible for West to refuse to take the ace if he has it. By giving him the count of your diamonds you will have created in his mind the very real fear that you might have started with two hearts and a singleton club, in which case ducking the club lead would allow you to make all thirteen tricks.

This may seem rather a light-weight hand to finish with, but it is a good example of the deceptive style that must be cultivated in order to score well at match-point pairs.